SHADOW OF THE RING

SHADOW OF THE RING

THE UNBELIEVABLE MR. BROWNSTONE™ BOOK SIXTEEN

MICHAEL ANDERLE

Special Thanks
to Mike Ross
for BBQ Consulting
Jessie Rae's BBQ - Las Vegas, NV

Thanks to the JIT Readers

Keith Verret
Diane L. Smith
James Caplan
John Ashmore
Jeff Eaton
Kelly O'Donnell
Peter Manis
Daniel Weigert
Misty Roa
Angel LaVey
Micky Cocker
Larry Omans
Nicole Emens
Paul Westman

If I've missed anyone, please let me know!

Editor
Lynne Stiegler

*To Family, Friends and
Those Who Love
to Read.
May We All Enjoy Grace
to Live the Life We Are
Called.*

CHAPTER ONE

F*amily is life. That, and brisket.*

James took another huge bite of the meat on his sauce-covered fork. The trays on the table in front of him were laden with piles of Jessie Rae's barbeque, neatly divided into smaller piles by sauce type. This was one enemy he was always willing to face.

Since Alison was on summer vacation, he'd made sure they hit Jessie Rae's at least every other week. Driving hours for good barbeque might seem extreme to some, but Jessie Rae's wasn't just *good* barbeque. It was the best.

PFW is heading the right direction, but we're still a long way off before we're even close to Jessie Rae's.

Alison sat across the small table working on a rib with the intensity of a starving wolf. She set her half-eaten rib down on her plate, a mischievous smile on her face.

"What's up?" James rumbled, a little nervous at her look.

"Have you noticed how I've been calling her Mom all

summer and she's stopped complaining and telling me to call her 'Aunt Shay?'" The teen grinned.

"She'll be your stepmom sooner rather than later." James shrugged. "And she loves you. There's no point in fighting it. Even Shay knows there are some fights she can't win."

"I know she loves me. I'm just happy she's letting me love *her*." Alison looked down with a wistful smile. "I have fun at the school, and it's been an interesting couple of years, but I miss you both when I'm there. Just chatting with you on the phone isn't enough." She sighed. "But I also miss my friends when I'm gone. It's confusing."

"There's nothing wrong with having people you actually like." James punctuated his sentence with a bite of pork.

Even though I know his ingredients, I can't match the taste. He says he's not using magic, but it's hard to believe that shit sometimes.

Alison stared out the window, a thoughtful expression settling over her face. "Makes me think."

"About?"

"The future." Alison shrugged. "I'm going into my junior year. Only one more year after that, and I'm done at the School of Necessary Magic. I don't have any big plans other than going to college."

James nodded slowly. They'd discussed this briefly on and off throughout the summer, and he didn't want to pressure her too much. His life path might not be the best for her. There were a few things that he'd prefer, though, even if they were selfish.

"You still thinking about a local school?" James nodded

at the window. "Local to LA, but you could go to school in Vegas without it being too annoying."

"I was thinking UCLA, actually."

"Really?" James gave her a thoughtful nod, although the idea excited him more than his barbeque. "You could live at home. Hey, you could take some of Shay's classes. That might be fun."

"We'll figure out where I'll live when I go, but I do like the idea of going to a school where Mom's going to be teaching. I'm not going to major in archaeology or history." Alison pondered that for a few seconds before appending, "I might minor in them, though."

"You do what feels best. I don't know shit about what you should do when you go to college." James grunted. "I'm still pissed that dick of a department head made her go to an all-day boring-ass meeting about the departmental budget. She would have been here otherwise."

Alison shrugged. "That's what it means to be a professor, Dad. Meetings. Lots of meetings, especially since she'll be teaching more than just guest lectures." She let out a happy sigh. "And don't worry about me. I've had a lot of quality time with her this summer since she hasn't been taking as many jobs, although I could have gotten some more in if you'd let me go on a job or two with her and Lily."

"You're ready for a lot, but not tomb raiding. It's too unpredictable." James surveyed the trays, wondering if he should go for another rib or return to the glories of the brisket. "At least when I take you on bounties, I've got a lot of guys around you. They can watch your back. Even if you've learned a lot of tricks with your soul sight and energy magic,

3

you're still blind. And that damned gnome is taking his sweet-ass time making those glasses to help you with that."

"I've lasted this long without seeing like normal people. I think I'll survive a little longer." Alison shrugged.

Mike, the owner of Jessie Rae's, stepped out from behind the counter and walked over to their table. "Everything okay, James?"

"Great." James lifted his fork and brisket. "Always great. Shit, I meant to ask you before. We don't have a date set for the wedding yet or even know the number of people, but I'll pay whatever you want if you'll cater the wedding. I'll also pay for whatever transportation you need once we know where it'll be."

Alison picked up her glass to sip her water, an amused smile on her face.

Mike gave James a skeptical look. "You know me, James. I'd love to cater any event associated with you, but are you sure that your fiancée wants barbeque at her wedding?"

James grunted. "I don't care what other frou-frou shit Shay wants at the wedding. I'm having barbeque, and I want the best barbeque on the planet. I'm trying with PFW, but they aren't there yet, and I don't think Shay's gonna put the wedding off for years."

"I'd be honored." Mike smiled. "When you've got some dates and guest counts, just let me know. I'll shut down this place for a week if I have to." He laughed. "Besides, catering for James Brownstone isn't exactly bad advertising." He held up his fingers as if framing an invisible banner. "I can see it now. 'Taste the barbeque so good, the Scourge of Harriken had it at his wedding.'"

Alison laughed, no longer able to contain her amusement.

"I just want to make sure there's halfway decent food at the wedding." James shrugged. "Weddings are long, and I don't want to be hungry all night."

Mike nodded. "Understood." He glanced down when his smartwatch buzzed. "I've got to check on something. Talk to you later." He headed toward the back and laughed. "Now I've got something to look forward to. I'm going to have to cook my best ever."

Alison giggled. "Seriously, Dad? Barbeque at your wedding?"

"You're damned right. I'm only getting married once, and I don't want to be hungry at it."

"Between you and Mom, everything's going to be so different anyway, you might as well. It's funny—I think I've had more barbeque in the last couple of months than I had all last semester."

James grimaced. "What are those pixies feeding you at that school? Oriceran kale?"

"It's good food, Dad. Just not barbeque most of the time. Really."

He nodded toward her plate. "There are good places in Charlottesville. I've taken you to some of them. You should hit them up. Didn't you say they'll let you leave campus once you start your junior year?"

Alison nodded. "Yes, they will."

James shook his head, feeling vaguely disappointed. He liked to think of himself as a good father, adoptive or not, but he was failing his daughter if she was barely eating barbeque most of the year. Some family traditions were sacred.

Good thing I planned this shit out better this summer.

Lyle whistled *If I Only Had a Brain* quietly as he approached the security line. He placed his briefcase on the conveyor belt and walked toward the metal detector, half-wondering if the DNA lock would catch the security personnel's attention.

Might be fun to let them freak out for a few minutes, but I'm on a tight schedule here. I've waited too long as it is.

Waiting until everyone else on his flight had headed toward the gate would make the entire process easier. Flying a red-eye out of a regional airport might not be as comfortable an experience as he would have preferred, but proper planning was necessary to avoid unnecessary attention.

He wasn't ready yet for exposure, which was why he'd chosen this airport. A regional airport wouldn't have decent magical detection resources.

Right now, the two agents manning the security checkpoint were his only concern. The bored and tired employees would be trivially vulnerable to his little tricks as long as he let fun overwhelm necessity.

One agent sat in a chair, staring at a laptop displaying the results of the X-ray scan. He frowned and stopped the conveyor belt. He glanced at Lyle, his eyes narrowed.

Lyle cleared his throat. "It'd be helpful if you just let that through and forget about what you just saw. Yes, I know what's inside, but you don't have to worry about it. I'll handle it. You probably don't understand what you're looking at anyway." He laid his hand on his chest atop the small bone charm on a chain hidden underneath his shirt and concentrated. The charm warmed up, and he smiled at the other agent. "And just let me through the metal detector. I'm going to miss my flight if you keep me here too long, and we can't have that, can we?"

The first agent started up the conveyor belt again, his eyes glassy—a victim of the bone charm's mind-control magic. "Okay, sir."

Lyle walked through the metal detector. It beeped, picking up the loaded .38 he had in a holster under his jacket. These days he considered guns crude and often unnecessary tools, but a man could never be too careful in an uncertain world. Someday he might actually run into someone immune to the magic.

The second guard waved him through, his eyes also glassy. "Just go ahead, and hurry it up. Don't want you to miss your flight, sir."

Lyle grabbed his briefcase with a huge smile. "Thank you. You two have made my day."

"What's in there, exactly?" the first agent asked.

"Just some special magical explosives," Lyle replied cheerfully. "You don't have to worry, though. These aren't intended for the plane. I'm just selling them to someone in Los Angeles. I think they need them for a coup or something somewhere. Who the hell knows? As for me, it's just a little mini-vacation-slash-business-trip. But forget that I ever said that. Forget that I was ever here once I leave. Can you do that for me?"

Both men nodded.

"Thanks. You're very helpful. I'll make sure to leave a positive review for you online." Lyle walked over and shook the second agent's hand. He was tempted to give him a new command and humiliate him, but making a big scene at a small airport would draw PDA attention he didn't need, at least not until he was ready.

It wouldn't hurt to test out a few things in Los Angeles while I'm there. This penny-ante crap is getting old.

Lyle continued toward the gate, ignoring the occasional weary and bleary-eyed traveler heading to the area. He finally closed on his boarding gate, where the ticketing agent was tapping at her computer.

She blinked and looked up at him. "Can I help you, sir?"

"Oh, I need to get on that flight." He beamed a smile at her.

The ticketing agent frowned and glanced down at her computer. "Sir, I'm sorry, the system says every ticketed passenger is accounted for. You sure this is the right flight? A lot of people get their gates mixed up with these red-eyes."

Lyle pointed at the large digital display listing the flight number and destination, LAX. "No, this is definitely the flight I need. Just let me ask you one question: is there an open seat?"

"Yes, but our airline has a policy about minimum time of arrival prior to boarding. They're getting ready to close the door. I'm sorry, sir, but it's a firm policy. It's a matter of security."

"Security's important. You never know what kind of freaks might be trying to get on a plane these days." Lyle reached up and pressed on the charm again. "You're going to call the plane and order them to let me board. There was a mistake in the system, and I should be let on. Do I make myself clear?" He kept his voice calm and pleasant.

The woman sighed and nodded. "I'm sorry, sir. I didn't realize there was a mistake in the system." She grabbed her walkie-talkie. "We have one more passenger boarding. VIP."

Oh, nice. I didn't even tell her to treat me like a VIP.

Lyle leaned in to whisper, "Once the plane takes off, it'd be helpful if you forgot about me. Can you do that for me…" he glanced down at her nametag. "…Deborah?"

"Of course, sir," she responded, completely glassy-eyed.

After the walkie-talkie crackled to life and urged his boarding, Lyle waved and headed down the jetway.

Those smug wizards at the club always thought they were better than me. Who needs their kind of magic when you have this kind of power instead?

They'd told him stories about mind-control magic, inherent to some creatures or accessible through wizard spells, but everything they'd mentioned required too much work, things like having to all but convince the person by normal means for it to work, but the bone charm just required him to give commands. He'd yet to encounter anyone who could resist it, magical or mundane. He'd even purposefully started a bar fight and then ordered the angry men to punch themselves in the head until they fell unconscious.

That was a fun night!

His personal favorite incident had involved speeding until a cop pulled him over. He had mocked the police officer and then ordered him to pants himself and cross the highway. Investigators had determined that magic had been involved, but they had no way to trace it to Lyle. He was driving a car he had stolen using the magic, and he had abandoned it that same day.

Lyle returned to whistling as he approached the door to the jet. The money he'd earn in Los Angeles would be only the beginning. The wizards had been right; before, he'd been nothing. He hadn't deserved respect, but the bone charm had changed everything.

The sin wasn't trying and failing. The true sin was not seizing the opportunity when it presented itself.

All those years running errands for those bastards and being their little lackey, and they never suspected I was paying attention. Never suspected I was waiting for a chance to take what I deserve.

The gates to Oriceran are open, assholes. Regular people can become special with the right artifacts, which is why I'm here and you're probably rat food.

Lyle snickered quietly. He wondered how long the wizards had survived after he'd used the bone charm to force them to blow each other's arms off with spells. For the first few weeks, he'd checked the news, but he hadn't seen anything. If they were still alive, they hadn't come looking, but he suspected they were rotting in the basement of the abandoned house where they had been trading illegally-imported artifacts.

A visibly annoyed redheaded flight attendant waved him onto the plane. The first-class section was small, just four seats, and only one was filled.

Lyle pressed the charm again. "You don't need to see my ticket. I am in first-class. Sorry for the delay."

The woman's pursed lips turned into a smile. "Of course, sir. Let's get you seated and get you a drink."

The difference between a king and a commoner was how people treated a man, and Lyle was tired of being a commoner.

What good is a king who doesn't have any permanent servants? Let's see what I can scare up in Los Angeles.

Lyle headed toward one of the spacious first-class seats and made himself comfortable.

A man across from him in an expensive-looking blue suit offered him a polite nod. "I hate red-eyes. I always think I'm going to be tired and nap, but I can never get to sleep." He laughed. "I can't complain too much. The company will pay for first class as long as I keep it under a certain amount, and I'm addicted to first class."

"Oh, I don't mind late flights," Lyle replied. "I kind of prefer them. Fewer people, and less crowded. It makes a lot of things easier." He fastened his seatbelt. "You're going to LA for business, then?"

The man nodded. "Business conference on techno-magic integration in supply chains. It's boring stuff. Logistics magic, that kind of thing. To be honest, I was thinking about doing a little sightseeing." He gave a sheepish smile. "Plus, there's someone I want to meet. I've heard bad things happen to you if you bother him, but maybe I'll get lucky."

"Who are you talking about?" Lyle leaned forward, interested. "Some big-name Hollywood actor?"

"No, nothing like that. The Granite Ghost lives there. You know, James Brownstone? I'd love an autograph, but it's not like I'm going to show up at his house. He'd probably throw me through a window." The man's expression implied that he might enjoy it.

"You're a Brownstone fan, huh?" Lyle looked the man up and down. "Don't seem the type. I've seen the news about him, but I don't really care much. I'm not into all that true crime stuff."

"To be honest, I used to not pay much attention, but after that stuff with the Council, I got kind of obsessed with all things Brownstone, and then all things bounty hunting." The businessman chuckled nervously. "I particularly started getting into all these high-end bounty-hunters. It's amazing, you know? Not just Brownstone, but all the class fives and sixes. There aren't that many of them, so you can really get to know them if you study them. It's like following sports for me." His eyes widened, and his breath caught. "Ever hear of the Wu family? They used to be my favorites." A sad look passed over his face.

"Should I have?" Lyle shrugged, his face showing his utter lack of interest, but the other man didn't notice.

"Entire family of high-end bounty hunters; a multi-generational thing from way back in the day. Used to hunt demons and weird crap in China that was hiding in the shadows even when magic wasn't back, and then their ancestors came over to America with all those guys who worked on the railroad. Anyway, the point is, they were involved in going after the Council. Terrible story. Almost all of them were killed when they took on the Council. Only two survived, two sisters. One of them quit bounty hunting and now works as a waitress, but the other one stayed in the family business. Her name's May."

Lyle grabbed the entertainment tablet from the seat pocket in front of them. "Being a bounty hunter is a dangerous business. It's not surprising that a lot of them die. This May Wu in Los Angeles, too?"

"Nope. She lives in San Francisco right now. I read online she headed to LA to poke her nose into that Silver Ghost stuff, but Brownstone cleaned that up, so she's probably back in San Fran." The businessman snapped his fingers. "Did you know Brownstone's daughter is going into the family business? She's worked bounties. I read that the other day. It's why I've been thinking about the Wu family a lot. Man, I hope they don't end up like the Wu family. That would be depressing as hell." He shook his head, concern all over his face. "But you're right. Bounty hunting is dangerous."

Lyle pressed on the bone charm. "Let's stop talking about this. I want you to grab that tablet and find the most brainless movie on it and watch it for the entire flight. If you finish it, you can watch it again until we land."

"Sure. Whatever you say." The man smiled and collected his entertainment tablet. "Thanks for the talk."

Lyle turned away with a frown.

Bounty hunters. They don't matter. Bounty hunters aren't going to come after me if there's no bounty. I'll have plenty of time to set up everything.

It might be fun to play around with James Brownstone eventually, though.

Lyle cracked a grin. Strength was meaningless when it came to dealing with him. He could control men's minds.

CHAPTER TWO

J ames crossed his arms and grunted as two new hires
fell from the narrow rope bridge into the mud below
with loud yelps.

"Keep going!" Royce shouted at the men. "If you fall,
pick your asses up and get through the obstacle course. If
you want to work for James Brownstone, you have to
prove that you've got what it takes, and that means never
giving the fuck up, no matter what." He pointed to the end
of the obstacle where a sweat-soaked Alison stood
drinking Gatorade. "A damned blind teenage girl is outper-
forming most of your asses. That should be fucking
embarrassing. Now move your asses before I have to walk
over there and kick you through the obstacle!"

Alison waved at the men and held up her bottle. "Come
and join us. It's very refreshing."

The men groaned and hurried back to the cargo net
leading up to the bridge. Other veteran bounty hunters,
including some of Trey's boys and the new hires who had
come in after the amusement park incident, hurried along

farther down the obstacle course, their muscle memory and fitness assisting them toward the end with ease.

Everyone had trouble with the obstacle course at first, but it was hard to be put through the paces by Staff Sergeant Royce and Maria and not end up fit and flexible, given enough time. A low-level bounty could turn physical and dangerous in an instant, and every man and woman who wanted to work for the agency needed to be able to deal with that reality.

No more Shorties, James thought to himself. *I'm willing to take a chance on people, but I want to make damned sure they are as prepared as possible when I send them out on jobs.*

Maria frowned from beside Royce. "I'm sorry, James. I know you wanted to experiment a bit with expanding hiring, but maybe we should stick to recruiting from security and ex-police, that kind of thing. Pretty high level of attrition with these guys McCartney sent over. No offense. I've got nothing against the guy, but he's a priest, not an expert on kicking ass. Well, non-demon ass."

James shook his head. "It's fine. You and Royce will whip them into shape, but not everyone needs to be an ex-cop and shit. If they make it through your training, it's fine. If they don't, too fucking bad. I promised him I'd give them a shot, but I also made it clear it'd be on them in the end to prove they were worth that shot."

Maria looked like she wanted to object again but nodded instead. She watched as one of the men near the end took on the optional salmon ladder. The contrast between the experienced bounty hunters at the peak of their physical fitness and the rookies was striking.

James glanced between Maria and the men near the end.

Even a lot of guys from AET couldn't handle this course.

At the beginning of the summer, Father McCartney had approached James after a sermon and pointed out that given how successful he'd been at turning Trey's gang into law-abiding and useful citizens, he might consider giving certain other people a similar chance. In particular, he recommended a few members of his parish who'd been down on their luck and were now interested in turning their life around, along with some other people Father McCartney had encountered through his community outreach, not all of whom were members of the church. The priest had already prefiltered for the men and women he thought had the greatest chance of success.

James agreed to the plan, the only condition being that anyone who came to his agency looking for a job had to be accepted by his existing senior staff and go through their normal training for whatever position they were interested in. He was running a business, not a charity, and if they weren't a net asset to the Brownstone Agency, they needed to go elsewhere. Father McCartney had no problem with that and had been sending people to the agency throughout the summer.

While complete success eluded the priest's and bounty hunter's project, the results were positive overall. Charlyce had gotten a few new assistants upfront, which was helpful for dealing with the administrative requirements of expanding business in both LA and Vegas. There was even some talk of sending someone to Vegas as a full-time administrative assistant. More new hires now formed the core of a permanent custodial and maintenance staff.

James liked not having to contract out. Every new person he added to the agency created additional risk, but having people from his neighborhood or who knew people he trusted helped keep more dangerous ones out. He still had Heather do a deep dive on every applicant, though, just to be sure. After having dealt with the insane alien hiring Shay to get at him, it wasn't paranoia to double-check everyone's background.

Most of the remaining new hires were interested in being bounty hunters, convinced that the job was the path to easy money. Half had already washed out, but the handful who had survived more than a few days of Maria's and Royce's intense training had impressed James. Even the current day's stragglers.

James pointed at one of the men scrambling up the cargo net. Cuts and bruises covered the man's hands, and his brow was furrowed in intense concentration. "That guy was delivering pizza part-time a month ago, and now look at him. Not fucking bad."

Maria shrugged. "He's fallen five times on the course today."

James nodded. "He might fall a lot, but he's now in better shape, and he still makes it through the course, even after falling. He's improved a lot. I respect that shit, but I also trust you guys. Anyone you think can't cut it, you let them go. If people are improving and might be useful on jobs after training, I want them, but if they're gonna be a liability, I want them out the door."

"Don't worry about it." Royce shook his head. "In the

Corps, I took all sorts of lazy-ass pieces of crap and turned them into real men and women I'd be proud to serve with in a warzone. A lot of people just need a good dose of discipline to reach their true potential."

"Sounds good."

"I'll whip the survivors into shape as long as they continue to show up." Royce gestured to two of the new hires who were closing in on the end of the course. "Ethan and Aiden are almost ready for a Vegas rotation. We're still working out the details with Trey, though. They've done a couple of level-one jobs with the more experienced guys, and they were cool under pressure from what the other guys said. I'm impressed by how well they've done, for guys with no law enforcement or military background."

James nodded as he watched the men. From the minute he'd brought in Trey's boys, he'd relied on Royce to handle the training. If the ex-drill instructor thought he could make something of a rookie, James had no reason to doubt him.

Ethan and Aiden leapt off the final obstacle to the applause of the veterans and Alison. Lachlan and Isaiah handed them Gatorade bottles from an ice-filled cooler.

I've come a long way from just checking shit on the app and seeing what's up.

Maria nodded, a pleased smile on her face. "I will say that despite my concerns about some of the newest recruits' fitness, things are working out better than I thought overall, especially with cohesion. That was my biggest concern."

"Probably because you spent so many years as a cop," James replied.

"Sure, but that doesn't make it any less of a real problem. I wasn't sure how the security guards would mix in with Trey's guys or any of the other new hires, but everyone seems to respect your original guys." Maria chuckled. "You know what they're calling them?"

"What?" James asked.

"Brownstone's Original Guys. Sometimes they call them Council Veterans." Maria nodded toward a few of Trey's boys. "None of the OGs are being arrogant assholes." She gave James a sidelong glance. "Keep this up, this city's going to end up pretty damned safe. We'll have to move somewhere else to find business."

"Maybe, but I doubt I'm ever leaving LA. Too annoying to learn where all the best barbeque places are in a new city." James considered that for a few seconds. "And we're already cleaning up Vegas, so no reason to move there."

Maria chuckled.

Every man or woman I hire means fewer bounties on the street. Never going to be bounty-free in a place like LA, but that doesn't mean we can't try for it. Fewer criminals mean less trouble for the cops.

"If you can breathe, that means you can get oxygen," Royce shouted at the stragglers. "Which means you can still move." He cleared his throat and turned to James, his angry demeanor vanishing in an instant. "Everything's been great with the anti-magic training, but every time we do another round, it reminds me that we need more magical firepower. Victoria's helpful, but she sticks to Vegas, and Zoe might be living with Trey, but she's just a supplier. Your priest friend have any stray down-on-their luck wizards or witches he can send our way? I can't say I'm an expert on training magical types, but I can at least make sure they're physically fit."

James grunted. "No, he doesn't know anyone like that. For now, I'll just keep the guys in anti-magic deflectors and anti-magic bullets. If we need something more serious, then that's something me, Trey, or Victoria will handle."

Cheers arose from the gathered bounty hunters and trainees as the last two stragglers finished. They collapsed to their knees a few feet later. James, Maria, and Royce walked toward the group.

"What a sorry-ass display," Royce offered, shaking his head. He was back in full DI mode. He nodded at Alison. "A blind teenager is better at this shit than half of you, and the only thing she has to worry about day-to-day is making sure her boyfriend doesn't get caught by her dad."

Alison rolled her eyes.

Everyone laughed except James.

What the hell? Is Tanner taking that damned train to town and sneaking into her room or some shit? Wait. Fuck, Royce is just joking.

Ever since Alison had admitted she had a boyfriend, James had resisted the urge to track the boy down and have a loud and threatening one-way talk with him. The struggle was worse on some days.

"Be fair, Staff Sergeant," Lachlan called from near the coolers. "Alison's gone on bounties. She ain't no rookie like these bitches. You can't compare them."

Alison grinned and shrugged, her cheeks reddening.

Royce crossed his arms. "So now the blind teenage girl isn't just better at obstacles, she's also better at doing the actual job. That makes everyone look worse, not better."

The OGs all laughed. Ethan and Aiden did as well. The two stragglers forced themselves to their feet, lifted their chins and squared their shoulders. The push had had its intended effect.

Royce gave them an approving nod. "We train your body on the course, but the body is just a shell. The mind and soul animate it. Most people don't fail because their bodies have given up on them. They fail because they've given up on their bodies. We will continue to push you until you can push yourself past any limits you thought you had. At the end of the day, the only person you have to do better than each day is yourself. Do I make myself clear?"

"Yes, Staff Sergeant!" everyone called in unison.

"Everyone hydrate and rest up for fifteen. We're going out on a run after that."

Several groans broke out, but this time, none came from the stragglers.

James was barely listening to Royce and the trainees as he focused on Alison.

Shit. I barely know anything about her boyfriend. Maybe I should learn more. That little bastard gets to spend more time around my daughter than I do these days.

He grunted. Shay had told him that he needed to give Alison a little space to learn how to handle herself in a relationship. He was willing to do that, even though the fact that she'd admitted to having a boyfriend proved how quickly she was growing up.

It wasn't like he needed to protect her from tragedy. Alison understood pain. Tragedy and pain had brought them together, but he was her father now, and he wanted to make sure she didn't have to deal with unnecessary emotional garbage while she was learning to control her powers.

Besides, if that Tanner punk broke her heart, James had an easy solution, which mostly involved punting the boy from a cliff into the nearest ocean. He was a wizard. He would survive. Probably.

James surveyed the trainees with a hungry grin. "Tomorrow, it's time for some more everyone versus Brownstone family tactical training. Being fit is just the first fucking step. The next step is knowing how to master moving and shooting while dealing with a real threat."

Even several of the OGs grumbled at the announcement.

Royce and Maria nodded in agreement, their cool gazes passing over the gathered bounty hunters and trainees.

This shit is coming together. I've got a good team here, and with Trey leading things in Vegas, we can probably get a good team set up there permanently sooner rather than later.

The Brownstone Agency might as well be an army. With James at their head, there wouldn't be anyone they couldn't take down. Sometimes to achieve peace you just needed to kick enough ass, and he couldn't think of any situation that couldn't be resolved with significant application of force.

Maria scratched her chin. "Inspiration."

Royce and James looked her way with questioning expressions.

"Everyone who came in with Trey has personally worked with you, James, on a job." Maria shrugged. "But a lot of the newer guys haven't, because these days you only take on fours and fives. I think it'd be good for the guys to see you doing your thing, not on tv or the net but in person. I know it's not worth your time, but even I busted the occasional low-level piece of shit when I was still in AET. It sets a good example. And I mean seeing you kick a bounty's ass, not *their* asses."

"Find me a good bounty or two who'll make a good example, then. One thing I'll never get tired of is taking idiots down." James slammed his fist into his palm. "And it's good to remind shitbags that they can't hide from me just by being low-level."

Maria smiled like she'd been given her favorite Christmas present. "Give me a day or two, and I'll find something really fun for everybody."

CHAPTER THREE

T his is what I get for not planning ahead, Shay thought.
She crossed her legs as she settled in at the
dining room table and stared down at her phone sitting
beside her plate and frowned. She didn't even care about
her sizzling steak. "This shit is annoying," she mumbled.
"I'm having one of those moments when I start thinking
like you, James. That freaks me out a little."

Alison gobbled down her steak, watching the two with
interest.

James looked up from his slab of meat. "Huh? What are
you talking about?" A faint hint of excitement filtered onto
his face.

Poor guy. He probably thinks I'm about to say barbeque.

"Keep it simple, stupid," Shay explained.

"I'm totally lost." James glanced over at Alison. "Do you
know what's going on?"

"Wedding planning," she mouthed.

"Oh." A wide grin from James followed.

Shay's head shot up. "What's so funny?"

"I spent all that time worrying about the proposal." James cut into his steak with the precision of a surgeon. "All that time I worried I was gonna fuck it up." He finished slicing off a piece and looked back up at Shay. "But now *you* get to feel the pain. You get to deal with all this annoying wedding shit. That's funny."

Alison swallowed a bite and chuckled quietly.

Oh, it's not gonna be that easy, James. Not that easy at all.

"*I* have to deal with the wedding shit?" Shay raised an eyebrow.

"Yeah. It's your wedding. Or you gonna use a wedding planner?"

Shay smirked. "Who says you don't have to deal with anything? It's your wedding, too, in case you forgot."

"Can't I just pay and let you make all the decisions? I'm a guy. It's not like we care that much." James shrugged. "I don't care about what color napkins we have or how the tables are arranged or any of that."

"*Pay?* I could pay for our wedding with the money I make from a lame-ass side job." Shay's gaze flicked back to her phone. "I'm fine taking point on this, but like I said, this is your wedding, too. Anything in particular you want? And don't you dare repeat how you don't care that much." She rolled her eyes and nodded toward his coffee table. "This place is so clean we could probably do a transplant in here without antiseptic. You might be a badass who loves charred meat, but you're anal as hell and obsessed with what you like, so you need to tell me what you want for this wedding. It's not like we're going to get a second shot at it, and I don't want to hear a bunch of bitching while you're walking down the aisle."

Alison hid her huge grin by drinking some water.

James blinked a few times, confusion spreading slowly across his face. After a few seconds, a look of forlorn resignation set in, but it was quickly followed by something else: hope.

"Barbeque," James declared. "Since you asked, that's what I want." He frowned at his steak as if irritated it wasn't ribs or brisket. "Not just any barbeque, but barbeque from Jessie Rae's. I already talked to Mike about catering it. He just said to give him the number of people and date, and he'd be ready. I'll handle all the transportation shit if you don't want to." He pondered the possibilities. "I wonder if Addie Endo could transport Mike and all the equipment and ingredients? Or shit, should I just buy all the equipment and ingredients and have them at the venue?" He furrowed his brow. "This is getting complicated, but this is one time I think I'll just have to put up with it."

Shay shook her head slightly, looking amused. "Barbeque, huh? And you're considering hiring high-end couriers to bring barbeque and pitmasters to your wedding? I'd like to say I'm surprised, but that's like the most predictable thing you've ever asked of me."

"Nothing wrong with being predictable. It keeps shit simple overall. Why? You don't want barbeque?" James' gaze flicked to Alison, but she ducked and chuckled.

He squared his shoulders. If his daughter wouldn't back him, he'd have to win the battle himself. There were some things that were non-negotiable in life.

"It's fine." Shay shrugged. "You're doing the hard part by getting the supplier, so we might as well make it a very

Brownstone wedding. I'm assuming you won't have a huge problem if we have other food as well? We can ask on the invites if they want barbeque or something else."

James furrowed his brow. "Can't we make the vegetarians bring their own food?"

Alison and Shay both laughed.

"I was thinking non-vegetarians who don't like barbeque," Shay explained. "Such people exist, you know. And I want at least *some* fancy food at this thing."

"You can have pizza at the wedding if you want, too." James grunted. "I don't care. Get all the fancy pizza you want."

"I'm not talking about pizza." Shay eyed him, unsure if he was joking. "I'll pick something a little classier for my contribution." She set her phone down, crossed her arms, and smiled softly. "It turns out you have a lot more opinions on the wedding than you've been saying these last couple of months, or even a few minutes ago, Mr. I'm-A-Guy-And-I-Just-Want-To-Pay-And-Do-Nothing- Else."

"Had too much time to think, so it's hard to not think about them. It's not a big deal or anything." James shrugged. "Just not going to be annoying about it."

"It's fine. Glad you give a shit. It means you're invested in this thing." Shay nodded at the phone. "But I'm not sure yet about most of the details myself. I always assumed I'd never get married, so it's not something I have put a lot of thought into. I do want something that involves fewer Special Forces soldiers and a venue not in the middle of a highway, but I'm not really clear on the details other than that."

James frowned, and Alison gave them a worried look.

They had been a little less than detailed on the exact nature of what had happened at the proposal. Shay had mentioned there were a lot of cheering people around, but she'd let the girl assume that it hadn't involved a military strike team.

Shay held up her hand to display the jade ring. "To be clear, I loved the proposal. It was what I wanted, and it was epic. I'm just saying I want the wedding to be slightly more on the traditional side. Not totally traditional, but at least a little closer."

James nodded. "Me too. I want Father McCartney to do the ceremony."

"Fine by me, but I'm telling you now, I'll agree to love, honor, and cherish, but obey?" Shay shook her head.

"Yeah, you shouldn't lie in a church." James sliced off another piece of steak and speared it with his fork. "And we both know you do whatever the hell you want."

"Like you don't?" Shay raised an eyebrow.

"It's worked for me so far." James downed yet another piece of steak.

"Same here."

Alison let out a contented sigh. "It's so romantic. A wedding! I've been waiting for this for a long time." She bounced in her seat. "And now we're talking about the details. I don't care if it's probably not going to be for a year, I'm so excited."

"You haven't been waiting *that* long," Shay replied. "It's not like we've known each other for twenty years."

James grunted.

Alison shrugged. "Percentage-wise, it's been a much bigger chunk of my life than yours."

"True enough, but it's also not like I'm that much older than you." Shay sent a playful glare at the girl, not sure if Alison was poking at her age.

Alison laughed. "Oh, that reminds me. Are you going to take Dad's name?"

James crossed his arms and his face lit with interest, obviously eager to hear the answer.

Shay shrugged. "I figured I'd hyphenate. A lot of useful reputation built up in the name Brownstone. Seems a shame to not take advantage of that." She winked at Alison.

"And weddings aren't romantic," James muttered. "They're complicated and require a lot of work. Most times they aren't simple. I should know. I've listened to a lot of podcasts. All the top ones on weddings." He pointed his fork at Shay. "Which is why I'm leaving it mostly up to her. It's not like hunting down a bounty." He lowered his fork. "You know, if we had the wedding in Vegas, we could just go grab some Jessie Rae's afterword. Ever consider that? Now *that* would be simple."

Alison stared at James, her mouth open. "Dad, are you serious? Or is this some sort of sad, sad attempt at a joke?"

James shrugged again. "Why not? I'm sure I can get Father McCartney to go there. I don't know all the laws and license crap, but if we look into it ahead of time, it won't be a big deal. People do it all the time."

Alison sighed and shook her head. "I keep having to remind myself that you're still learning about women in so many ways. You're the biggest badass in the United States, or maybe the world, but you're more clueless than some of the boys at my school."

"Huh? What do you mean by that?"

I better nip this in the bud damned quick.

Shay gave James a death stare. "I'm not having some quickie wedding in Vegas." She crossed her arms. "It's going to be epic, just like the proposal. A touch more normal, though, even if I'm still figuring out the venue. And the theme. And everything else." She shrugged. "But keep in mind that this is one bridezilla you won't beat in a fight."

"What's the budget?" Alison asked. "That's a good place to start planning from."

"Budget?" Shay snorted. "Screw the budget. It's not like I need to build another fifty warehouses. Between your dad and me, we can spend whatever we want. Sure, not gonna buy an island or something, but other than that, we can go anywhere." She furrowed her brow. "Maybe even Oriceran."

James shook his head. "I want to stay on Earth. Probably get jumped by some angry Council lackeys or Laena fans if we went to Oriceran. Can Father McCartney even marry us if we're on another planet?"

Shay shrugged. "No clue."

"Earth's fine." Alison smiled. "And since you have no budget limit, you should go crazy." Alison gasped. "How about a cruise ship?"

"Cruise ship?" James frowned. "What do cruise ships have to do with weddings?" His frown deepened. "Does the captain have to marry us then?"

"You could charter an entire ship for the wedding and make it a wedding on the waves." Alison bobbed her head. "This is genius. You should do it."

"A cruise ship, huh?" Shay thought it over for a few seconds. "A huge cruise ship might be pretty epic."

"Until it sinks." James frowned. "Boats sink."

Shay and Alison laughed.

"We just have to make sure we have enough lifeboats," Shay suggested. She tapped the cruise ship idea into a note on her phone. "Gonna collect like twenty of the best ideas, and we can thin them down from there."

"Glad this wedding isn't happening anytime soon," James mumbled. He furrowed his brow. "Hey, while I'm thinking of it, Shay, Maria is looking around for a good bounty that I can go do to inspire the guys by demonstrating ass-kicking. You interested?"

"Inspire the guys?" Shay made a face. "That sounds like you're going to kick some level twos through a window or something."

"Might punch them through a window." James smirked. "Probably won't be dead-or-alives, so I won't kill them. Just wanted to ask if you wanted in."

Shay shook her head. "Nah, you have fun. If something more serious and high-level comes up, let me know. Still waiting for Peyton to find me a decent tomb raid before the summer ends, too."

James looked over Alison. "What about you?"

The teen sighed. "I don't think I should come along."

"Why?"

"Dad, I might be blind, but I also have powerful magic and can sense souls and magic and all that. I think the guys might get a little discouraged if I go in there and throw a spell or something that knocks out a bunch of guys." Alison smiled.

"How is that different from me punching a guy through a window?"

Alison laughed. "You don't get it. Even if you're stronger than a normal man, it's just more of something they can see themselves doing. It's inspirational. It's not like Drow shadow magic. Does that make sense?"

"Okay, if you don't want to come, that's fine. You've already done several bounties this summer."

Shay smiled. "We'll have a girl's day while you're kicking low-level ass. Just let us know when."

"Okay, will do."

Shay grinned. "And now back to wedding planning."

Later that night, James knocked lightly on Alison's door. "Alison, you still up?"

"Sure, Dad, come in," she called.

James opened the door and entered. Alison sat at her desk, her fingers running over her adaptive Braille reader. He wondered what she was reading.

Alison set the reader down and turned to face him. "What's up, Dad?"

He shrugged. "I just figured we should talk about stuff. I wanted to make sure everything's okay with you. You're going back to school soon."

Alison smiled. "Everything's great. Why wouldn't it be?"

"Trying to keep the lines of communication open." James made air quotes around the last few words and scraped at the floor with his boot tip. "Something they said on one of my podcasts. Everything going okay with that *boy*?" He grunted.

"'That *boy*' has a name, Dad." Alison rolled her eyes. "Tanner. You don't forget anything, so I know you know his name, and you'd like him if you met him."

You're damn right I know his name, and his smug little face.

"Just asking."

Alison leaned forward and tilted her head. "And you're going to keep your promise?"

Even if she couldn't see his face, she could see his soul. A lie would be painfully obvious, but a little clarification wouldn't hurt in case she gave him the opportunity to handle the situation in his preferred manner.

"Promise about what?" James asked.

"Going Overprotective Brownstone all over Tanner." Alison crossed her arms and straightened her back. "If I recall, there was a clear promise made that you wouldn't go, and I quote, 'menace' Tanner if you happened to bump into him when you dropped me off."

James grunted. "Fine. I won't as long as everything stays the same and he doesn't give me a reason."

"Keep in mind a valid reason will be determined by me, not you." Alison blew out a breath and relaxed her shoulders. "Good, that's all I needed to know. I'm not a little kid, Dad. I wasn't a little kid even when we first met, and now I also have decent control of my magic. It's not like you have to protect me from everything in the world."

"You were planning to meet two shady gangsters in an alley by yourself when I first met you." James snorted. "That sounds like a little-kid move."

"I could have handled them. Seriously, you have enough

faith in me to take me on bounties, but you act like I can't be trusted around boys. A level-three witch is way more dangerous than a boy."

James shook his head. "Not a teenage boy."

Alison frowned and stared at him.

"Okay, okay. I know you're not a little kid, and that you're growing up." James shrugged. "Doesn't mean I have to like it."

Alison stood and walked to James. She wrapped him in a tight hug. "No matter what, though, I understand that all you want to do is protect me. I love you, Dad."

James patted her head. "I love you, too, Alison."

She pulled away. "And I can't tell you how happy it makes me that you're getting married. Even though I already thought of us as a family, this will make it official."

"I'm glad you're happy, but keep in mind, it might not happen for a while. My best guess would be next summer, but she might push it out further." James checked over his shoulder. "Sometimes I think Shay likes to make things complicated. I mean, who needs five warehouses?"

"Well, the system kind of makes sense." Alison looked at him earnestly. "There's different stuff in each one with different security requirements."

"Just saying. I guarantee that if I get out of this wedding only having to worry about a cruise ship, that'll be the simple and easy option."

Alison arched a white eyebrow. "What do you think's going to happen?"

"I don't know. Maybe Shay has us ride in on a glider and parachute onto some magic island that only appears once every twenty-five years, or we end up on the moon in some gnome-supported magical bounce-house."

"Gnome-supported magical bounce-house?" Alison burst out laughing. "Dad, it's her wedding, not some little kid's birthday, and there aren't any gnomes on the moon." She frowned. "I don't think."

"I don't know." James lifted a shoulder. "I'm just along for the ride now. I'm only concerned about one major problem."

"What is that?"

"If the location is too out there and weird, we'll have to bring in supplies by portal." James frowned. "Not sure how portal magic might affect the God Sauce, and I don't think Mike would know."

Alison smirked. "I'll ask Professor Cooper when I get back to school. He's an expert on portals."

"What about barbeque?"

"I'm sure he's eaten barbeque at some point in his life."

James nodded slowly. "That's better than nothing."

CHAPTER FOUR

S o this is what they mean about being careful what you wish for, Shay thought. Or is it more of a "hoist on your own petard" deal? No, definitely the first.

She tilted her head as she stared out the living room window, her phone to her ear. "Push Smite-Williams, then. He's always got some big shit he needs help with, and it's not like I need a forty-million-dollar payday. I just want a job that's not a total waste of time."

"You sure you want me to call him?" Peyton replied, uncertainty in his tone.

"Yeah. I'm sure. Why wouldn't I be sure?"

Peyton sighed. "Because you're right about him and jobs, and that's the problem. If I ask him, it's not going to be a simple one-day job. It's probably going to be at least a day in travel alone."

"I know, and I want something major." Shay sighed. "I'm not saying this is my last hurrah or anything, but it's probably going to be my last major job until the winter. I've beaten Alan down to the point where the university has finally hired me as a full-time professor, and now I have to teach normal classes during fall semester."

"I thought that was what you wanted? I'm really confused now."

Shay chuckled. "It's not a big deal. Just get me something. I want to scratch my itch so I can concentrate during the semester. Make sense?"

"Yes, that makes sense," Peyton replied. "I think."

James looked up from petting Thomas.

Shay closed the blinds after a quick check for anyone suspicious. She didn't like that James left them open a lot of the time. He might always have Whispy Doom on him, but he didn't always have the symbiont bonded. An accurate sniper or a rocket launcher would have a good chance of taking him out, and it wasn't like he didn't have a whole world of enemies.

For that matter, he had multiple worlds of enemies.

It's a good thing that his reputation is scaring everyone off now. He's tough, but if someone knew how his powers worked, they could win.

She sometimes wondered if she wasn't paranoid enough anymore. If she'd gone soft from living with a very hard man, ironically. She'd caught herself not practicing defensive seating when they went to restaurants. If she ended up getting shot in the back, she was going to be so embarrassed in the afterlife.

Oh, I see, you were a former professional assassin who got shot in the back. That's like a chef dying from food poisoning.

"I do want to focus more on teaching going forward, Peyton." Shay headed to the couch. "But I'm trying to be realistic about my damned schedule. I won't be able to jet away in the middle of the semester. That's part of the compromise that comes with trying to be a real person with a real job instead of a phantom tomb raider who only semi-exists behind a code name."

Peyton blew out a breath. "Kind of weird to imagine you teaching people. The only thing weirder would be...I don't know, maybe James becoming a cat guy?"

"I've been giving guest lectures for a couple of years now." Shay frowned. "You helped set up my fake records so I could do that, and now you're saying you don't think I should teach?"

"I didn't say you shouldn't teach. I said it was weird. You're not grading anyone during those guest lectures or having to deal with people trying to get out of stuff." Peyton laughed. "I can kind of imagine you throat-punching some student because he said your lecture was boring. Or, someone comes to you and asks to reschedule a test, and you're all, 'I didn't get to reschedule when those gang members tried to ambush and kill me, you lazy sonofabitch.'"

Shay glared at her phone. "Keep it up, and I'll drive over there and start my throat-punching with you."

James chuckled from his seat.

"Just saying," Peyton replied. "Also don't college professors have to be calm? Or at a minimum, not threaten their brilliant employees with violence, even jokingly?"

"Calm? A little bit. At least until I get tenure, but that might be too much. And I *am* calm. These days I don't automatically kill everyone who tries to kill me. How can you say that's anything but calm?" Shay snorted. "Besides, your problem is that you only ever deal with me in one context. I don't need to threaten or hurt anyone at the school. People actually find what I have to say about revised history and archaeology interesting, and it's easy to slip in tomb-raider tidbits and attribute them to someone else, so even if anyone asks, it's easy to deflect. It's the perfect position for me."

"The whole thing is still weird," Peyton stated. "But I'll keep looking around for something that works. I'll send you a message if I find something for you job-wise. I wouldn't want to get throat-punched. I've grown accustomed to my trachea not hurting."

Shay snickered. "Remember, I was joking about that. Mostly. Talk to you later, and thanks, Peyton."

"No problem."

She ended the call.

James glanced at her. "Everything okay? Lot of talk about throat-punching. Is he pissing you off?"

"Not really. He's just stating the obvious, and I don't want to hear it." Shay shrugged. "I'm changing my lifestyle again in a complete and huge way, but otherwise than that, it's fine. Nothing to worry about."

"You sound freaked out." James looked concerned.

"I'm really not." Shay smiled. "I'm just a little unsettled. I don't know. Tomb raiding was always kind of a short-term plan. It wasn't something I was planning to do for the rest of my life." She slipped her phone into her pocket. "I was supposed to save up enough money to go hide on an island somewhere until I was old and gray, but now that plan's gone. Switching from full-time tomb raider to part-time professor and part-time tomb raider isn't as weird as it could be, all things considered."

"It'll involve fewer throat-punches." James grunted. "And bounty hunting can be annoying, but it's got far fewer strange creatures."

"I go to out-of-the-way places that have been touched by magic. A weird creature or two is to be expected. As for the throat-punching, I'd hope I'll need it less, but it depends on the class." Shay chuckled. "I'm not going to give the raids up entirely. I'm just cutting down on them. Probably hit one decent one per season."

James nodded. "Is there anything that would make you give tomb raiding up entirely?"

Huh. He's super-inquisitive today. I should probably encourage him to ask shit when he's curious, so I don't have to spoon-feed him so much other stuff.

"Interesting question." Shay gazed into the distance for a moment. "I honestly don't know anymore. Sometimes I think I've made enough money, so why bother, but other times I know I'd miss the excitement. Once I've been off for a few months, I really get the urge. It's not just the adrenaline rush, but being the first person to lay eyes on some ancient magical artifact in centuries. That makes it hard to give up. What about you?"

James frowned. "What *about* me? I'm not a tomb raider. I help you out when you need it, but I don't really give a shit about historical artifacts even if they are magical. If it's useful, that's different, but useful for a bounty hunter is not the same thing as useful for a lot of other people."

"Yeah, I know you're not a tomb raider, but you've slowed down on your bounties, too."

James grunted. "Not a lot of high-level bounties are dumb enough to come near me these days, and the agency handles all the low-level shit, so it's not like they need me either. That gives me free time."

"There's an entire world full of shitbags out there." Shay gestured grandly with her arms. "Or at least the rest of the country. I know you hate flying, but you've made road trips before, so I think you slowing down isn't just about how you and your guys are cleaning up LA and Vegas. There's something more here."

"Shit's simpler when it's close to home." James glanced down at his now-sleeping dog. "And I've got other reasons to not go running around everywhere like a coked-up rabbit chasing a carrot that's flying away."

"Okay, that was an interesting image." Shay laughed. "What reasons?"

"You and Alison. And barbeque. PFW's becoming more than just some shit we do when we have time. A restaurant on the side isn't a crazy idea anymore."

"Of course. Luckily I'm not a vegetarian." She gave him a playful smile.

James grimaced at the mere thought. "Some shit's not funny. Fancy-ass restaurants are one thing, but I'm not eating some eggplant bullshit that someone is trying to pretend is the same as meat. They are *not* the same. That's why people eat meat."

Shay couldn't pass up the opportunity to tweak James a little.

"Don't tempt me," she replied. "Maybe I should try a week with no meat. Bella's trying it out. She says she's a lot more relaxed."

"Bella doesn't have to tomb raid," James rumbled. "And

the best pizza has meat. You gonna stick to vegetarian pizza?"

Shay considered that for a few seconds and laughed. "And thus ends my brief flirtation with the dark side."

"Good." James shuddered.

Shay snickered. She remembered James telling her how someone had once cornered him at a barbeque competition and tried to convince him that their grilled cauliflower "steaks" were better than anything else there. He had complained that he didn't know how to deal with that level of delusion.

Some things have changed, but in all the main ways, you're the same man as when I met you.

Shay leaned forward, honest curiosity in her eyes. "To be clear, I'm not asking you to stop bounty hunting, James, especially since I'm not stopping tomb raiding. I want that to be clear. But we're planning our future together, and I want to just pick your brain about what you've been thinking about, so we're both going in the same direction."

"I don't know. I'm doing more with the barbeque competitions since I have more time. I'm glad I didn't do much extra shit this summer so I could spend time with Alison." James shook his head. "I don't think I'll ever stop, not completely. There will always be some level five or six out there who needs his ass kicked, and Whispy and I might be the only ones who can do it."

Shay's smile slowly faded. "I've been meaning to ask you. Have you heard from Johnston lately?"

"The senator?" James shook his head. "Why?"

Shay scoffed. "I don't know. I'm just surprised by how

all that shit went down. Between all the weird alien-related government black projects and assholes like Durand, I half-figured some fuckers from the CIA or something would be busting down your door and trying to drag you to some black site for alien captives in the Bermuda Triangle or wherever the government stashes that kind of person."

"They're welcome to try," James replied, his grinding voice even lower than usual. "And I'm welcome to beat their asses. If I've taken down this many bounties and nanoforms, there's no reason to be worried about the government, but I don't want them to be put in a bad position either."

"'Bad position?'"

James nodded. "I'm not gonna fight the military or the cops."

Shay frowned. "If the government ever realizes that, they could use it against you. Keep that in mind."

"The government's got to realize it'd be a dumb move. It's too risky, and could backfire on them."

"They're the government, James." Shay shrugged. "You can't trust them."

"I *don't* trust them. I just figure that by this point, they know not to fuck with me. If they throw soldiers at me, I'll escape and find the fuckers who'd risk those men's lives and make them pay for it," James growled.

Shay thought that over before giving a slight nod. The local AET had come around before seriously going after James, but she could still easily imagine some corrupt government bureaucrat deciding that James Brownstone was a problem to be "solved."

What would he do if they gave him no choice? If the soldiers had been lied to?

Shay kept her face calm even as her stomach knotted at the scenario. Whispy Doom was powered by anger and rage. James had learned to control and harness that rage at a slow drip, but if anyone ever pushed him too far, they might face the true wrath of a Vax.

I need to protect him and make sure that never happens.

Shay furrowed her brow. "I wonder if we should have Peyton and Heather using their tracking shit more. I don't think the government realizes just how much we know about their surveillance. I've got more of those anti-tracking spell artifacts coming, too."

"I think we're fine. What the government is doing isn't worth stopping. They want to waste taxpayer money on that shit, fine by me. We should save our surprises for when we need them the most. Besides, Senator Johnston saved our asses from the Nine Systems Alliance." James shrugged. "I don't mind letting him and his buddies provide a little free backup if we need it in the future."

"I wouldn't worry about Aiyn's buddies. I doubt they're coming after you again, not when the choices are basically risking war with Earth and Oriceran or leaving you alone."

"If they do return, they'll back the fuck off, or I'll make them back off." James narrowed his eyes. "I'll fight every fucking asshole from every planet in the galaxy if I have to. I'm not letting anyone push me around."

"Let's try and keep the galactic warfare off the table, at least until after the wedding."

"That's up to them, not me."

James phone buzzed and he pulled it out.

Shay eyed his phone. "That's not some NSA warning

where they're all, 'Don't talk shit about the government, we're listening,' is it?"

James shook his head. "Just Maria scheduling an ass-kicking. Supposed to be inspirational and shit for the men. Did you need me for anything tomorrow?"

"Nope. Feel free to run wild."

James' thumbs flew across the touchscreen.

Shay snickered.

James looked at her. "What?"

"I just like how we went from talking about you basically threatening the entire galaxy to casually arranging with one of your employees to probably go violently empty a warehouse full of mobsters." Shay smiled. "Don't ever change. I'll admit, for all my bitching at times, I like the man you are."

James shrugged. "I can't be anybody else."

CHAPTER FIVE

Lyle leaned back, enjoying how the leather of the Porsche's seats molded to his body. He half-wondered if some sort of magic was involved in production.

I should have gotten one of these a long time ago. I always tried to tell myself expensive cars weren't that much nicer, but damn, do I love this car. Too bad I can't keep it.

He assumed that someone would eventually find the body of the car's previous owner and immediately start looking for the vehicle, but he'd planned to switch vehicles soon anyway.

Even ignoring the security issues, for some reason, the red color wasn't doing it for him. He had been in a gunmetal-gray mood the last few weeks. A quick trip to the dealer might be in order.

No. Too many cameras there, and new cars are too easy to trace, but there might be someone around here with a car I want. This is a nice neighborhood.

Lyle's car moved slowly down the street as he surveyed

the houses in the area. They were all large, with large fenced-in yards. They'd be considered expensive homes by any normal standard, but they lacked the grand presence he desired to match his new status in life. The proper man needed the proper car and the proper home to show off who and what he was.

He frowned. The only reason he was in that neighborhood was to make a multi-million dollar delivery, which immediately brought other questions to mind.

Given how much money this guy's going to pay for my package, I'm surprised he's not living somewhere more impressive. This looks like upscale-office-drone country, not ridiculously-rich-asshole country.

Lyle sighed. A mansion might be more appropriate for his current tastes, but anyone who lived in a mansion probably had enough connections that simple mental domination or disposal wouldn't work out well. Especially since he still wasn't certain of the limits of the bone charm's power.

I need to experiment with more subtle conditioning. I wonder if I could get someone to do something long-term without me being around? That could be handy. Or I can just get enough money that I can pay people to not give a shit no matter what I do around them. That might be easier.

Lyle chuckled as he parked the Porsche on the street near a huge gate. He wasn't there to get a new house. He was there to make a delivery. The money would help kick-start his new life. Hiding in hotels with his powers or grabbing free dinners had been fun, but it was a waste of his potential now that he had access to true power.

I wonder if this is how some of the guys did it back in the day.

Lyle reached into the backseat to grab the briefcase and exited the car, then walked over to the huge wrought iron gate and glanced at the keypad on the panel beside it. He pressed the call button and waited.

I hope this guy's home. I've got better shit to do than wait around all day. Maybe I should just rob a bank? No, that won't work. Too many cameras. Go to some brokerage and get them to transfer me a bunch of money?

"Can I help you?" came a gruff male voice over the intercom, breaking Lyle out of his thoughts.

"I'm here to see Mr. Sarkazian. I have his delivery." Lyle held up the briefcase. There would be a camera somewhere watching him. "This is the address I was told. I was also told to make sure I mentioned Travis sent me."

There was no response for ten seconds. Finally, a loud buzz sounded, and the gate unlocked.

"Come to the front door," the voice commanded. "Don't make any sudden movements."

The same could be said for you.

Lyle pushed through the gate with a smile. He used to be so unhappy. Every day, he'd wake up and think about how the world had screwed him over and pushed him into a life he'd never wanted, but now he understood that had just been a test. Since he'd proven himself, he'd been given the bone charm and the chance to make his life whatever he wanted as long as he worked hard.

How could a man not be happy in that situation?

Lyle meandered up the red-brick path that wound through the vast well-maintained lawn. A few orange trees broke up the monotony, but the landscaping wasn't very interesting.

At my future mansion, I want something cool. Maybe a hedge maze, but a killer one like in The Shining. *Some Oriceran should be able to make that if I pay them enough. Or it can be an attraction. I could charge people.*

He chuckled as he arrived at the front porch. He took a moment to smooth the lapels of the new suit he'd taken from the same man he'd taken the car from. The suit fit looser than he would have liked, but he couldn't argue with the price. After his payday, he could go buy himself an expensive hand-tailored suit.

The door swung open and a huge, muscular man jerked his head toward the inside. "Hurry up."

Lyle entered and smiled at the man. "Great sunshine today, am I right? Such nice weather you've got here in LA."

The guard grunted, and his nostrils flared. "Who gives a fuck about the weather?"

Lyle clucked his tongue. "If you can't appreciate the world around you, what's the point of living? What separates you from a machine? Ever think about that?"

"Just get in the fucking living room." The guard glared at him.

"Fine, fine." Lyle continued out of the foyer, slowing for a moment to appreciate the intricate weave of the carpet.

Need to get me a bunch of fancy carpets. And tapestries? Are tapestries still a thing rich people have? If not, maybe I can revitalize the trend.

Lyle followed the guard into a huge living room filled with leather couches and paintings. A massive curved table of frosted glass sat in the center of the room.

A few nice tables, too. Definitely need those.

He had no idea if the various landscapes and portraits were worth anything, but they did seem like something a rich asshole would keep in his house.

What am I thinking? After this deal, I'll *be the rich asshole.*

A silver-haired man stood near the wall, staring up at a painting of sunflowers, his hands behind his back and resting on a cane topped with a blue crystal.

Wonder how expensive that *was?*

Lyle cleared his throat. "Good afternoon to you, sir. I've come a long way to deliver your package. You're Mr. Sarkazian, I presume?"

The other man turned. The decades had lined his face, but he retained much of the handsome visage of his youth. "Yes, I am." He nodded toward the table. "Enough pleasantries. Show me."

"Of course, Mr. Sarkazian." Lyle walked over to the table and set down the briefcase. He placed his thumb on the DNA scanner and grimaced. For all his new-found power, he couldn't do anything about the burn. Fortunately, this would be one of the few times he'd need to deal with a DNA lock.

Soon it'll be people coming to me and saying, "Yes, sir. Here's your delivery, sir."

The lock clicked, and Lyle opened the briefcase. Dozens of small plastic bags filled with multi-colored crystals were piled inside.

Suspicion on his face, Sarkazian looked Lyle up and down and walked toward him, leaning heavily on his cane. His unsteady gait made it clear he had some sort of knee problem.

Wonder why a rich guy like him doesn't get it fixed?

"There you go, sir. Premium stuff," Lyle explained. "It's not easy to smuggle these crystals off Oriceran. Of course, the extra difficulty and inherent danger have to be reflected in the price."

At least that's what those wizard assholes said.

"A reasonable stance." Sarkazian nodded to his guard, and the other man walked into a nearby hallway and disappeared around the corner. The older man sat on a couch and laid his cane across his thighs. "Such destructive power, yet so stable. How very useful."

Lyle pulled out his phone. "I've got a QR code with the number of the relevant account. When we last talked about this, you said TrollCoin would be fine. If you want to pay another way, we can discuss that, but I would prefer TrollCoin."

"I was surprised when you contacted me. I've been dealing with those wizards for a while. They've been useful for getting me things I need."

"I'm sure they'll be able to deal with you directly again soon, but they've sent me in the meantime to provide all the services you need," Lyle lied. "I'm not a wizard, but I strive to be useful."

"Aren't you going to ask?" Sarkazian stared at him as if judging him.

Stop looking at me like that. You don't understand who you're dealing with.

"Ask what?" Lyle's smile finally dimmed as suspicion played across Sarkazian's face.

"Aren't you going to ask what I need the crystals for?" Sarkazian pointed his cane at the open briefcase. "Most people would at least be curious why I needed an entire briefcase full of magical explosives."

"Not my problem, as long as you pay. I'm a business-man." Lyle injected more energy into his smile. "If anything, knowing what you want to do with them is a disadvantage."

"I used to be like you," Sarkazian replied quietly. "I used to think nothing mattered but money. I spent my life obsessed with gathering it, not paying attention to the moral or ethical considerations. But the other things *do* matter."

Lyle's curiosity finally got the better of him. "The crystals aren't to take down your local competitors?"

"What sort of local competitors do you think I have who would require this sort of solution?"

"You're a guy who can pay millions for smuggled explosive crystals. I'm guessing your enemy would be some sort of organized crime group." Lyle held up a hand. "Like I said before, I don't really need to know the details, but since you asked, yes, I'm a little curious. Not judging, mind you. All I'm here to do is deliver them to you."

"What if I told you I intended to kill normal people with them?" Sarkazian's cold, dark eyes fixed on Lyle. "Not criminals, just innocent people minding their own business."

Man, this guy has so much money, but he doesn't know how to enjoy life. Too bad.

"Normal people?" Lyle made a face. "Why do you need this sort of stuff for that? If you just want to kill people, why not just use guns or normal bombs? The great thing about Earth is that you don't need magic to kill people."

Sarkazian shook his head. "I need to prove a point about how evil magic is, and to do that, I require magical items. Do you understand now?"

Lyle groaned. "Oh, you're New Veil." He waved a hand and gave Mr. Sarkazian a sheepish smile. "I have to admit I actually feel kind of dumb here. Of course, a bunch of terrorists would want explosives. Duh. Blowing up Mafia guys with magical bombs would attract too much attention." He shrugged. "For some reason, I just assumed you were normal criminals. Not weirdo hypocrites."

"Hypocrites?" Sarkazian narrowed his eyes.

"Yes. Come on, killing people with magic to prove magic is evil is kind of weird to me. If anything, it just proves humans are the real evil or whatever." Lyle shrugged.

"We do what's necessary to save this planet."

"I honestly don't care. You can do whatever terrorist anti-magic shit you want. That's your business. All I care about is getting paid. I'm not really a political type of guy, you know? So, can we just get on with the payment, already?"

The guard from before stepped back into the room, flanked by three other men. They all had handguns out.

"We'll get on with something else." Sarkazian glared at Lyle. "Who are you really? FBI? Hmm? PDA? CIA?"

"That's a lot of letters." Lyle chuckled, his heart as calm as before. Sarkazian had made a mistake by not killing him instantly if this was how he wanted to play it. That had been the man's only chance to win. "I'm a businessman, not a government guy. And I was honest earlier, I don't care what you intend to do with the crystals. I just want to get paid. This doesn't have to end poorly."

Sarkazian picked up his cane and smashed the top against the table so hard he left a web of cracks. "You think I don't know this is a setup? You think I'm a complete fool?"

Lyle sighed. "Are you going to pay me or not?"

"If you tell me the truth, we might consider keeping you alive. If you don't, we're going to get the truth out of you, however long and however painful it may be." Sarkazian stood, resting one palm atop another on his cane. "Traitors to reality must be punished, and those who refuse to join our side are traitors, whether or not they support magic."

"You know what the real problem is with you New Veil types? You're fighting a losing battle. I mean, what's the point? You think you're going to somehow stop magic? You know what they say: you can't stuff the genie back in the bottle." Lyle laughed. "Probably a genie who came up with that. Wait, are genies real?"

The four thugs advanced on Lyle, their guns trained on him.

"Your arrogance is about to bring you a lot of pain," Sarkazian stated. "I'd be lying if I said I won't enjoy it."

Lyle clucked his tongue quickly twice. "You're going to make things complicated for me, aren't you? Oh, well. At least I already have everything I'll need to clean up." He pressed on the bone charm underneath his shirt. "The first guy in the room, point your gun at the head of the man who came in after you. The next two point your guns at each other's heads. The last guy, point at the first guy's head, and all of you wait for further instructions."

The bone charm warmed against Lyle's chest.

Sarkazian frowned. "What are you trying?"

The four thugs complied, their guns now turned on each other and their expressions blank.

"Not trying, doing," Lyle explained. "Everyone with a gun, pull the trigger." Three of the thugs' heads exploded. "Last guy, kill yourself."

A loud gunshot followed, and the last man fell to the floor.

Lyle smiled at Sarkazian. "I just wanted to test that. In movies, they're always able to resist suicide commands. Huh. Guess that shows you the difference between movies and real life."

The older man's eyes widened. "You *are* PDA, aren't you?" He laughed. "Go ahead and try it on me, then, you wizard piece of trash. You'll be disappointed" He sneered.

"I'm not a wizard, and I don't work for the government. I used to work for wizards. You know, the guys you were dealing with originally." Lyle smirked. "Too bad they were such idiots that they were supplying dangerous gear to anti-magic terrorists. See, that's why they're dead now: because they were idiots who underestimated me. Just like you. Now hit yourself on the head with that cane."

Sarkazian didn't move except to grin. "You're not a wizard? Then you have some sort of toy?"

Lyle frowned. He hadn't run into anyone who could resist his power yet, magical or otherwise. His gaze dipped. The crystal on top of the cane was slightly cloudier.

Shit. I didn't know anti-magic deflectors came in different colors.

Lyle frowned and walked toward the older man. "You

think I can't take down an old man?" An invisible force field stopped his forward movement. "What the hell?"

"I've collected more than enough artifacts to beat wizards. That's what it means to be a member of the New Veil. Hypocrisy, you might call it, but it's really polluting ourselves to save Earth." Sarkazian chuckled. "You should have never come here, but whatever artifact you're using will be of great value to my group. Don't worry, more of my friends are on the way."

"Hit yourself with the cane," Lyle ordered. "Bow before me. Get up and try to dance."

Sarkazian's smirk grew wider. "You're stubborn, but that's not admirable, only pathetic."

"Count to twenty. Count to thirty. Tell me what thirty-four times fifty-seven is. Call up your last contact and tell them to go fuck themselves."

The bone charm grew hotter. It was now uncomfortable against Lyle's skin.

Huh. Never had to try this hard before. This is interesting. Glad this guy proved a little harder. It's better to know my limits before I run into someone who might actually be trouble.

Sarkazian burst out laughing.

Lyle continued rattling off random orders, focusing on the darkening of the crystal on top of the cane. The other man didn't seem to notice.

"Don't you get it?" Sarkazian shouted. "You can't win against me. Run, little man. If you run right now, you might be able to escape before my reinforcements arrive, but we'll still chase you down and make you pay for your arrogance."

Lyle ignored him and continued rattling off quick commands.

Sarkazian stood up and glared at him. He lifted his cane. "You don't have a shield, do you? Just because I have a bad knee doesn't mean my arm doesn't work."

"Bend over and kiss my ass," Lyle replied. "Donate five hundred dollars to an Oriceran Resettlement Charity. Give your car away to the first bum you see. Go on television and challenge James Brownstone to a fight."

The crystal was now black.

Almost there. Now who's the arrogant asshole?

The terrorist hobbled forward. "You should have run when you had the chance."

"Give me the cane. Hit yourself with the cane. Throw the cane away."

Sarkazian raised the cane.

"Hit yourself in your bad knee with the cane," Lyle suggested.

Cracks shot through the now-jet-black crystal and it shattered, the pieces raining down on the carpet. Sarkazian gasped and stumbled back, shock on his face.

"This mind-control stuff is pretty hefty magic," Lyle explained. "You shouldn't have assumed your little crystal would hold. Now let's test if it was also responsible for the shield." He walked forward until he was right in front of the other man. "Looks like the answer is a big yes."

Sarkazian tried to bring down the cane, but Lyle's hand shot up and grabbed the other man's arm. He curled his free hand into a fist and slammed it into the terrorist's stomach.

The older man gasped for breath and fell to his knees.

Lyle smashed his fist across his face and Sarkazian dropped to the ground, his face bloodied.

Messing with their minds is fun, but beating someone up is fun, too.

Lyle sighed and scratched his eyebrow. "I should take the crystals, but it's more trouble than it's worth. I really just want the money." He knelt in front of the other man with a bright smile. "Here's what we're going to do. You're going to transfer all the money you can to me, and then you're going to sit here for seven minutes after that. When those seven minutes are up, you're going to activate one of these crystals. That'll probably set the rest off, but do you understand?"

Sarkazian's eyes grew glassy, and he nodded slowly. He pulled out his phone. "Is TrollCoin okay?"

"Yes. That'd be peachy." Lyle grinned. "It's a pleasure doing business with you, Mr. Sarkazian."

Lyle glanced down at his watch, then into his rearview mirror. He wasn't sure if he'd be able to see anything from so many blocks away.

A massive orange-red explosion erupted behind the car. The ground rumbled, and the car rocked.

"Damn!" Lyle shouted. "That probably took out half the block." He laughed. "So much for being subtle, but that was so damned cool."

Lyle threw back his head and laughed. He had let fear rule him too much. Yes, he had to be careful that someone didn't surprise him, but as long as they didn't, he would always win—just like Sarkazian had found out.

He grimaced. "That was a nice house. Maybe I shouldn't have had him blow it up."

Lyle started whistling, *If I Only Had a Brain* and let his mind wander. A king or emperor could order a man to do something, and they might do it, but only out of loyalty or fear. Lyle could order a man to kill himself, and the man would comply because he had no choice.

That made Lyle more than a king or emperor.

You know what? I'm a god, and it's time to start collecting worshippers.

James frowned at his phone. He lifted his head to look over at Maria, who was sitting across from him at the conference table. "You sure? Not even a single level three. It's organizational, but that's not gonna make much of a difference if they've got a wizard hiding there or something."

Maria nodded. "Remember? That's the point. If we keep it low-level, the guys don't have to concentrate on guarding their asses, so they can watch you do your thing. You're right, it's a level-two organizational bounty with a lot of level ones mixed in—mostly dust dealers and petty muscle. This group's independent, so it's not like we'll create any waves when you take them out."

"Don't give a shit about creating waves. If there's a bounty, that's enough. What did Trey say?"

"I just got done talking to him on the phone right before you showed up, and he agrees this is good." Maria chuckled. "He said, and I quote, 'Sounds like a good moth-erfucking curb-stomp for the big man.'"

James picked up the phone again to stare down at the bounty notice. When he'd first started bounty hunting years ago, he'd concentrated on low-level bounties. Even without using his amulet, he hadn't had much trouble, and he'd quickly graduated to focusing almost exclusively on higher-level bounties. By the time he'd met Alison, it wasn't worth it to even go after level twos. In recent months, he'd stuck to level fours or higher.

"Fine. I'll do it, but I want everyone ready. You never know when some easy job will involve some fucker with an experimental CIA grenade."

Maria smirked. "Ah, yes, the infamous naked Brown-stone incident."

James grunted. "Don't call it that."

"That's how Shay always refers to it when it comes up."

James scoffed. "You two talk about that shit?"

"Sometimes." Maria grinned, too much excitement in her eyes for his comfort.

"Whatever." James stood. "Just get everything set up. Let's get this bounty crap taken care of. If we wait too long, some asshole level-five will probably roll into town and cause trouble."

CHAPTER SIX

James slammed the door of his F-350 closed and frowned at the rundown warehouse. The problem with scumbags was that they always hung out in crappy places. Assholes never had any pride.

Engage stronger enemies for maximum adaptation, Whispy whined. *Projected adaptation minimal. Achieve maximum adaptation to achieve primary directive.*

The amulet had been bitching the entire trip over. Apparently, Whispy didn't understand the concept of inspiring the men. The only thing important was making James stronger.

Achieve primary directive? Which one? The one where I sell out the planet, or the one where I waste every other Vax symbiont who shows up?

The amulet radiated irritation. *Continuing adaptation in progress.*

That some sort of status report?

From what James understood, Whispy had spent the last few months modifying him. It wasn't totally clear what had been involved, but he was regenerating a lot faster, and his blade and energy blasts were both stronger.

Maximum strength necessary for all possible primary directives, the amulet noted.

So you don't care as long as I fulfill one of them?

Primary directive conflicts noted.

James chuckled. The slamming of car and SUV doors echoed as the men and women from the Brownstone Agency finished stepping out of their vehicles. Every single bounty hunter wore a tailored black suit and an anti-magic deflector over a concealed bulletproof vest that added only the barest amount of visible bulk underneath their shirts. Everyone carried a stun rifle in their hands and a stun rod clipped to their belts, along with a holstered conventional sidearm.

Someone moved in the second-floor windows of the warehouse. The enemy knew they were there

Good. If they get all set up, this will make for a better show for everyone.

Rapidly eliminate all enemies, Whispy demanded.

Sure, I can do that shit. Then we can both be happy.

Maria checked the power cell status of her weapon before turning to face the others. "Remember the general plan. We're going to follow James and pick up any of the stragglers, but let him be the tip of the spear." She pointed toward the fence behind the warehouse. "The OGs have set up on the opposite side. If anyone tries to run, they will pick them off, so you get the fun of going through the front entrance and watching the master at work. Also, remember that this is not a dead-or-alive bounty either for the organization or any of the individual bounties." She gave James a long, meaningful look. "Clear?"

James shrugged.

"So stun them," Maria continued. "Or knock their asses out. Don't kill anyone unless your own life is at risk. Are we ready to clean up a dust ring and make a lot of money?"

"Yes, ma'am!" the bounty hunters shouted.

Maria walked over and leaned forward to whisper to James. "We need a good show, but will you be able to take out all these guys and not kill them without using your full armor?"

James grunted. "Don't worry. This shit's gonna be easy."

"Okay. Lead on, then."

James didn't bother to draw his gun as he marched toward the gate in the center of the fence. The bounty hunters fell in behind him, their guns at the ready.

Heavy chains connected to thick locks secured the gate.

"Should I go get some bolt cutters?" asked a man.

"No," James rumbled. He backed up and charged the gate. His shoulder slammed into it, and the chains jangled. After another two tries, the left side of the gate flew off its hinges and hit the ground with a resounding crash. "See, we didn't need any bolt cutters." He looked down at the chains still connected to the lock. "Good chains and good locks, but they need a better fence."

The bounty hunters laughed.

Ethan jogged forward. "Mr. Brownstone, I've got a question."

James glanced his way. "What?"

"Aren't you concerned about the lack of surprise? Even

if they somehow hadn't tagged us before, they definitely know we're coming now."

James shook his head. "A lot of the time, I *want* assholes to know I'm coming." He tapped his forehead. "The lower the bounty, the greater the chance he's a cowardly piece of shit. I've got a rep, and now the Brownstone Agency has a rep, and you can use that to make shit simple. The goal should always be to get the bounty, and if you can do that by scaring the shit out of them, might as well." He glowered and stomped toward a side door. "If they know you're coming, they have more time to think about it. Sometimes they'll get scared and overreact, but if you're prepared and *not* scared, it doesn't matter. They'll make all the fucking mistakes, and you can take them down."

The heavy steps of the mass of bounty hunters walking in near-formation echoed between the decaying buildings and sheds positioned around the warehouse.

"It's different for high-level bounties." James narrowed his eyes as a shadow moved in one of the first-floor windows near the door. "A level four or five has enough power that they usually either have a decent reason not to be scared or will be so fucking cocky they won't give up even if they're outgunned. And if they have a stupid-ass nickname, it's only gonna be worse. With those kinds of guys, you go in hard and fast and take them down before they have a chance to fuck you up." He threw up a fist to indicate that the group should stop. "Let me open the door. It might be trapped."

James reached for the door handle and turned. It wasn't booby-trapped, but it *was* locked. Unsurprising. He pulled out his .45 and put several rounds into the lock before holstering the weapon. A quick tug opened the door.

A frowning thug with a shotgun stood on the other side of the door, and he pulled the trigger. With a roar, the weapon spewed a slug straight at the bounty hunter, who was less than a yard away.

The round didn't even sting, but it did tickle.

Near complete adaptation previously achieved, Whispy reported, undercurrents of annoyance in the amulet's thoughts. *Eliminate useless enemy.*

The thug on the other side blinked and fired again. James stood there and let the man empty all five slugs into him. At the end of it, he had five new holes in his shirt but only the barest hint of redness.

Surprised gasps swept the crowd of bounty hunters behind James.

Maria smirked. "Seeing is believing, right?"

James took a few steps forward until he was right in front of the thug. "It's your lucky day, asshole."

The man swallowed. "I-it is?"

"Yeah. We don't get any money if I kill you."

James glowered at the man and, with a quick grab, tossed him through the door. The thug landed hard on his arm, crying out. Three bounty hunters dropped on him like piranhas, pinning his arms and securing him with zip-ties before he even had enough time to fully register that he'd landed.

The entrance hallway ran straight toward the main storage area on the right. Shouts sounded from both directions, but there were more voices coming from the right.

Clear out the main group and then pick off the stragglers. This is why low-level bounties annoy me.

James stomped down the hallway to the right with a feral grin. He might not have bothered under normal circumstances, but Maria wanted a show. If anyone asked, he wouldn't deny he was having a little fun.

Two men rushed around the corner, assault rifles in hand. The guns spewed bullets in full auto, further shredding James' shirt but barely scratching him. He didn't have a reason to bring extra equipment against a group of low-level losers, so the gray coat and tactical vest he would have otherwise worn had been left behind.

Maria and some of the others rushed in beside him.

Shit. Better not take too long. Somebody might get hit if I play around.

James charged with a loud bellow, and one of the men dropped his gun and ran. The other kept up until he got a first-hand introduction to James' fist.

The poor bastard flew back several yards and rolled another couple after hitting the ground before finally coming to a stop. He groaned, on the edge of consciousness.

A dozen tables had been set up in the main warehouse to form a sort of dust-processing assembly line. Boxes filled with baggies containing the colorful powder were stacked on a table farther into the room, with a station for cutting the dust with razors and mixing it with various liquids in bottles on other tables, a drying table, and a final table to cut and pack the final product into plastic bags.

James almost admired the efficiency of the whole operation.

The large number of men who normally worked the stations now crouched or stood behind other overturned tables, crates, boxes, and even the dusty remnants of a crane in the corner, all armed with a rifle, shotgun, or pistol. Even SWAT or AET teams would be threatened by the show of force.

James stepped forward and cracked his knuckles. "You haven't fired yet. Good. That means you aren't total fucking dumbasses. If you surrender right now, maybe you'll live through this. Otherwise, no fucking guarantees, assholes."

The seconds ticked by, with James convinced the fight was already over. He was disappointed.

"Smoke his ass!" screamed one of the thugs.

Hot lead blasted from across the room. Bullet after bullet struck James and bounced off. His already damaged shirt was reduced to a few scraps of fabric, and his pants were now more appropriate for a fashion-forward punk rocker than a barbeque-loving bounty hunter.

The sustained volleys stung slightly, but they hadn't pierced his skin—or if they had, Whispy was regenerating so quickly that James didn't even notice.

Engage stronger enemies for maximum adaptation, Whispy suggested.

James roared and charged toward the nearest gunmen. The buzz of stun rifles sounded, blue bolts blasting throughout the warehouse. A few men groaned and dropped to the ground, victims of the stun attack, but their cover had saved the bulk of the thugs.

One of the gunmen went for a grenade on his belt, but

he wasn't fast enough. James backhanded him into another man hard enough that both fell to the ground unconscious.

"Hurry up!" shouted a thug hiding behind an old refrigerator to another unseen man.

James ran in his direction.

A few other thugs dared to duck out from behind their cover to take shots at the rest of the Brownstone bounty hunters. The luckiest thugs only took four stun bolts at one time. Most took more. More than a few thugs experienced a severe failure of their bladder control.

James closed on the refrigerator, which was chugging along at a good but leisurely pace.

A thug jumped from behind the old appliance with an RPG launcher over his shoulder. "Suck on this, bitch."

At least it's not some CIA shit.

The RPG roared away from the launcher. James broke into a sprint, not even trying to dodge. The projectile exploded against him, blinding him for a second and leaving a few minor cuts and burns over his body as well as minor pain, but all of the wounds started to heal immediately. The amulet was fully exposed now.

James growled more for effect than out of anger as he yanked the launcher out of the thug's hand and batted the man away with it. The bounty hunter spun and slammed his makeshift weapon into the stomach of another man. The second thug collapsed to the ground, clutching his stomach and coughing up blood.

"Shouldn't give me anything this heavy and large to hit you with." James picked the man up and threw him into another group of thugs nearby, knocking them over like bowling pins.

Several dropped their weapons and ran, deep panic on their faces. The bounty hunters nailed most of them with their stun rifles, but a few of the criminals made it out the back door.

James rounded on the ones who were making a last stand.

Got to give them credit for keeping it up after everything they just saw.

One thug kept firing while screaming at the top of his lungs. Another man shook the entire time but managed to keep pulling the trigger. A few others stood there with resigned looks on their faces as they fired their rounds.

The bounty hunter didn't charge them. Instead, he slowed, taking careful steps and growling the entire time. The thugs kept shooting.

Blue stun bolts came from either side of James and sent the men to the floor.

He looked around for more thugs, but everyone in the main warehouse floor lay on the ground, unconscious or groaning.

Ethan and several others surged toward the back, rushing after the escapees.

"Don't bother!" Maria shouted. "The OGs will clean that shit up." She gestured around the room. "Secure all the existing prisoners. We have to sweep the warehouse for holdouts."

Ethan shouldered his rifle and whistled. "Was that for real?"

Maria knelt by a bounty and secured his hands. "What do you mean?"

The rookie bounty hunter pointed at James. "He took a missile from a rocket launcher, for fuck's sake."

"Technically, it was a rocket-propelled grenade. Slightly different."

James chuckled. He was a little charred, but not in any pain anymore.

Find and engage stronger enemies for maximum adaptation, Whispy insisted.

Ethan's gaze rested on the amulet half-sunken into James' now-exposed chest, the tendrils under his skin obvious.

"You're not just a badass," Ethan observed. "You're a force of nature." He pointed at the amulet. "We going to get one of those eventually?"

James shook his head. "Trust me, you don't want one. They're annoying most of the time."

Maria grinned at Ethan. "That doesn't mean you can't work your way up to some nice artifacts. Trey can almost solo level fours now."

Ethan blinked. "Really? And he went from guys like this to that?"

"Yeah." James shrugged. "Everyone's got to start somewhere."

CHAPTER SEVEN

S hay took a sip of her wet martini. "You keep asking James to do shit like that, he's gonna get a big head. I know he's a badass, but at least he's not insufferable about it." She took a moment to check around the crowd in the Black Sun. Tonight's group was more upscale, mostly higher-class criminals in suits and nice dresses, fashionable underworld types rather than gang members or street hustlers.

I used to worry in a crowd like this. Now I wouldn't care if an entire group of cartel enforcers came in.

Maria gulped some beer from her bottle. "It was good for the guys. And it's Brownstone. Sure, he can change, but he's not exactly the kind of guy who's going to become a diva over beating minor dust dealers down. That's like an NBA player getting more arrogant because he can dunk over junior high kids."

"I suppose you're right." Shay laughed. "Maybe I should have come along, too."

"No offense, Shay, but you're great when someone

needs their ass kicked, not so great when you need a lot of people alive afterward." Maria shrugged. "We were looking for powerful, inspirational, and non-lethal."

Shay shrugged back. "Can't claim I'm always good at not killing people. Inspirational? Seeing James beat down thugs is inspirational? I would have figured seeing him do that sort of thing would convince the regular guys they were kidding themselves about what it means to be a bounty hunter. It'd be like they couldn't reach him or shit like that. I don't know. I just have Peyton and Lily, not some huge staff I have to worry about."

"No, you have to think like a guy." Maria set her bottle on the table and gestured to a passing man. "When they see a badass, a lot of them instantly imagine themselves as that badass. It's all inspirational. I used to see it all the time in the LAPD: leadership by example. A good alpha male can be very inspiring, as long as he's not a dick otherwise. Brownstone might not exactly be the master of social niceties or subtlety, but he gives a shit about his job and his people. The men sense that, so when they see him also being badass, it inspires them. They don't resent him or themselves; they just want to be like him."

"Huh. Makes sense." Shay sighed. "Just keep me in mind. I have to live with him, but you're right. I haven't heard him say anything about it."

"Hey, I accepted that Brownstone was a ridiculous badass a long time ago. You can't fight reality, and since you're marrying him, you should as well." She looked over her shoulder. "Where is your fiancé, anyway? When you texted me to come out for a drink, I assumed he'd be coming along. There aren't any level fours or fives in town, and he had his fun the other day."

"He's having a daddy-daughter-night thing with Alison. They're out playing mini-golf, actually." Shay smiled.

When she'd met James, he had been so closed off. The only living things he had given a damn about were his priest, the kids in the orphanage, and his first dog, and the Harriken had killed his pet. It had been like he was a bounty hunting machine, barely existing, and his one reason to care about getting up each day had been taken from him.

While Shay would have liked to have claimed credit for awakening the man within, in truth, Alison's love had opened the door. Shay had just stepped through it later.

I'm pretty sure I fell hard for him before he did for me, but I have him now, and we both have a lot of reasons to get up in the morning.

"Mini-golf? That's surprisingly non-lethal and non-dangerous sounding." Maria furrowed her brow. "It's not like explosive mini-golf or something like that?"

"Nope. Just standard-issue putt-putt mini-golf. Alison's actually halfway decent at it."

Maria nodded. "She doing that magic pulse trick? You know, like she does when she runs the obstacle course?"

"Yeah, same basic idea. She wouldn't be able to pull it off at long range for normal golf, but mini-golf is just close enough that it works. We've gone a few times this summer."

"I'm less surprised by a blind girl going mini-golfing than I am by James Brownstone doing it." Maria's face scrunched in concentration, and she laughed. "I can see him threatening an obstacle blocking him."

Shay laughed hard and hit the table. A few people looked her way with frowns.

"He totally does!" she replied. "The last time we all went together, he was all like, 'I will fucking end you if you block this shot, you asshole windmill.'"

Maria chuckled. "What happened after that?"

"He got a hole in one."

"Of course, he did."

Shay nodded. "Anyway, I actually suggested James take her. She loves it when they do cutesy shit together, but she's not always forceful enough, and she doesn't make it clear what she wants. She thinks she's training him to be more thoughtful, but even if she can see into his soul, I think she overestimates how quickly he can pick up emotional cues." She sighed. "But it's not like he's not thoughtful. If anything, he can be *too* thoughtful."

"Too thoughtful?" Maria raised her eyebrows in question.

"Yes. Because he's clueless about women or girls in a lot of ways, he ends up focusing on the wrong stuff. I made him sweat with the proposal, but the truth is, the best strategy when you're dealing with him is to just be straightforward. Once he has a clearly defined target, he knows how to handle it." Shay shrugged. "And he handles it well."

"And is that what you did? Just told him to take Alison out to mini-golf because she'd like it?"

Shay grinned. "Well, I've found that I can often get

James to do certain shit on his own in the future if I frame it a certain way."

"And how did you frame it this time?"

"I gave him a big line about how it'll help her judge distances better in case she ever needs to throw a grenade."

Maria laughed. "I think he forgets she's a teenage girl at times."

"No, he never forgets that. Just ask him about her boyfriend sometime." Shay held up a finger. "The problem is that he doesn't really distinguish between what a grown bounty hunter male should do versus a teenage girl. To be fair, though, neither do I. I was doing nasty stuff when I was her age, so it only seems natural for us to train her."

"You're the weirdest family I've ever known, but somehow you make perfect sense together."

"Yeah. We do." Shay set her drink down and shrugged. "I'm also not sure which of them misses the other more when she's off at school. That girl's lucky."

"Um, aren't you lucky, too?" Maria eyed Shay. "You're marrying him." She gestured to the jade ring.

"Yeah, but…that's different." Shay sighed and shook her head. "I've told you about my shitty childhood. Hell, I just alluded to it. We both know what *that* led to. I'm not gonna apologize for my earlier life, but I'm not gonna pretend I'm all that proud of it either."

Maria's face tightened and she gave a shallow nod.

"And I didn't even have any magic," Shay continued. "Imagine if Alison had gone through all that shit without James. If she'd even survived the Harriken, her powers might have awakened in a vicious way." Shay stared into her glass.

"She might have found out she had a talent for killing and enjoyed it, but instead, she found James, and she's happy. She's got friends like a normal teenager, even if they are all magical, and she goes to a magic school. All thanks to James."

Maria frowned. "Hey, don't discount your part in this. You've known her basically as long as James, and you helped deal with the Harriken, too. I know you've been trying to resist it, but that girl sees you as her new mother."

"Yeah, but it's because of him that we have any connection." Shay shook her head. "Don't tell him I told you this, because again, he doesn't need a big head, but I'm not sure I'd be this...normal if it wasn't for him. I'd probably be barely better than I was when I first left my old job."

"I don't believe that." Maria crossed her arms. "You'd left your old job before you met him. You already knew it was a dead-end."

"And I was just marking time until I could retire away from people. I didn't give a shit about anyone or anything." Shay shook her head. "I just didn't want to die in my kitchen, murdered by my own friends."

A drunk man stumbled into Shay, knocking her hand and spilling some of her drink.

Shay frowned and glared at him. A couple of years back she might have broken his arm for that, but she didn't want to make any trouble for James or violate the neutrality of the Black Sun. Messing with Tyler didn't bother her all that much, but these days messing with Tyler effectively meant making Maria's life harder, too.

But does it count as a neutrality thing if some asshole bumped into me?

"Hey, you're hot," the man slurred. He grinned at Maria.

"You, too. Lot of hot chicks in here, but I like 'em athletic, and you both look athletic."

The back of Shay's neck tingled. She realized the reason. The entire bar had gone silent. It was as if they expected her to take the man down.

He's an idiot, but he hasn't done anything worth getting the shit kicked out of him yet.

Shay pointed to her drink. "Can you watch where you're going?"

"Come on, baby. Don't be that way." The man's gaze flicked between the two women for a second, and he grimaced. "Shit." He put his hands out. "Fuck. I didn't realize who I was talking to. Sorry. I've had a lot to drink. I'll go pay for a new drink." He rushed toward the bar.

Chatter resumed around them.

Maria sighed in relief. "I was enjoying my drink. Tyler always gets so pissy when there's an incident. He whines about it for days, and when I point out he could just run a regular bar without so many criminals visiting, he complains about business opportunities."

Shay shrugged. "I didn't invite you here to watch me kick some drunk's ass. I invited you here to ask a favor. I've been dancing around it, but I might as well get to it."

"A favor? What?" Maria frowned. "I don't do tomb raids. Fuck all those bats and spiders and crocodiles and crap." She shuddered.

"I don't need you for a tomb raid." Shay snickered. "I need a maid of honor."

Maria stared at Shay. "Not that I'm not flattered, but what about some of your other friends? You've known them a lot longer than me. Like Kayla or Bella?"

"I've known *them* longer, but they haven't really known *me* longer."

"I'm not following you."

"They're my friends, and I hang out with them, but as far as they're all concerned, I'm nothing but a feisty archaeologist who has had a series of rich boyfriends, continuing with James." Shay shrugged. "And as much as I've calmed down in the few years, it's not like any of them will ever be ready to know the truth about my past or even the tomb raiding. It's just not safe for them, even though I'm sure they'd all find it interesting."

"You not inviting them to the wedding? I don't want to cause any drama."

Shay shook her head. "No, I'm inviting them. They'll be bridesmaids. I already asked them, and they're all really happy about it. It's just, knowing you have my back and I don't have to lie to you will make this shit go down easier once I get it all figured out. You're the first female friend I've had, Maria, who I can be completely honest with and who isn't a professional killer—and a couple of those female killer friends tried to kill me."

"That's a weird distinction, but I'll take it." Maria lifted her bottle. "I've been to tons of weddings, but I've never been a maid of honor before. I'm kind of like you. Lots of guy friends, especially cops in AET, not as many women friends." She took a sip. "If you need help with anything, just let me know, and I'll do my best." Her eyes shifted to the side and a sly grin appeared. "You know, all this wedding talk has got a certain bartender-slash-information broker nervous. *Very* nervous."

Shay looked over her shoulder at Tyler. The man was busy preparing a drink and didn't even notice her.

"Really?" she asked.

"Yeah. Every once in a while, he'll idly ask me something about you and Brownstone and if I think you're going into this too quickly. It's obvious he wants me to answer yes."

"Too quickly?" Shay rolled her eyes. "We're not teenagers who just started going steady after prom."

"I know, I know." Maria waved a hand. "It's all just a cover for his own insecurities. He's worried I'm going to start sniffing around for a ring. Now he sees every interaction between us under the shadow of the ring." She pointed at Shay's engagement ring. "Every once in a while, I mess with him a little. I start hinting at it, and then I'll reveal I was talking about something else entirely."

"And how do you really feel?" Shay raised an inquisitive eyebrow. "You pretty much live with him now."

"I like him. Do I love him?" Maria shrugged. "Hell if I know. I think we both need to spend more time adjusting to our new lives."

"So you're not hoping for a ring from Tyler?"

Maria offered an evil grin. "Not yet. It's too damned entertaining watching him squirm. I hope it takes him a while before he works up the courage, but I'm not going to say I can't see a future between us." She sighed. "Fortunately, he's not that interested in kids. It's not like it's come up a lot, but I did idly mention something to him once about how I sacrificed motherhood to be a cop, and that I was too old now." She stopped and stared at Shay. "Have you discussed that with Brownstone?"

"Kids?" Shay shrugged. "We already have a kid. Alison."

"Yeah, but maybe he wants a new one?"

"Trust me, any kid not named Alison is the last thing on his mind."

You don't get it, Maria. He's not even human. Whispy might have rearranged him a little, but he's an alien who just looks human.

Huh. Maybe that's why he's never even brought it up. Oh, well. We both have Alison to keep us busy.

Shay turned again to look at Tyler. This time he noticed her and frowned, his eyes darting back and forth as if he suspected the women were plotting against him.

"The dominoes will really start to fall once James and I fully pull the trigger," she mentioned.

"Have you thought about a date yet?" Maria asked.

"Yeah, but I haven't come close to deciding. I know I want it to be in the summer so Alison's not at school. I'm leaning toward next summer. A year isn't too long, and it should give us plenty of time to get all this shit figured out."

"And Brownstone doesn't have any crazy ideas for the wedding?" Maria nodded toward the big-screen tv on the wall. "He's not planning to do some sort of big battle royal or something, is he?"

"No, he just wants a bunch of barbeque served at the wedding. He doesn't mind if we serve other food, though."

Maria laughed. "That's not so bad. Depending on who you invite, they might prefer barbeque over some sort of fancy chicken or fish."

"Maybe. His only other requirements are that his priest

does the ceremony and that it not be conducted on Oriceran."

Maria lifted her bottle to her lips but paused. "Not on Oriceran? Did you want to have your wedding on Oriceran?" She took a drink.

"No." Shay shook her head. "The idea just came up when we were discussing things. Honestly, I have no fucking idea what I want, and now I feel kind of bad for what I put James through with the proposal."

"Maybe instant karma is a real thing."

Shay smirked. "Karma for a tough proposal but not for my first career?"

"Didn't you mostly take out pieces of shit anyway?"

Shay thought that over for a few seconds before nodding. "You have a point." She polished off the rest of her martini and took a deep breath. "I have a lot of thinking to do. I'm not even sure who I'm going to invite. I probably should figure out that first."

"Probably. Unless you want to do a spite wedding."

"'Spite wedding?'"

"Yes." Maria nodded. "It's something a cousin of mine did. She had a wedding and invited several people she liked and a lot she hated, and then purposely sat them at shit tables in the back during the reception right next to the speakers and that sort of thing."

Shay scoffed. "I tend to kill the people I hate."

"That's another way to handle it."

CHAPTER EIGHT

*I*t's a great day to be alive, Lyle thought. *A very great day to be alive.*

He whistled as the glass doors slid open, and he stepped into the office building. He waved at the security guard. "How are we doing today? Great weather, am I right?"

"Great weather, sir," the man responded, his voice a near monotone and his eyes glassy. "Excellent weather, sir."

"I'm really loving the weather here. I should have moved to LA years ago." Lyle clapped once. "No wonder this place got so popular." He snapped his fingers. "Wait, you remembered to eat and sleep this time, right?" He shook his head. "You won't do me any good if you don't eat and sleep. You're my main man. My favorite security guard."

The man gave a quick nod. "Yes, sir. I did. Thank you for asking."

Lyle patted him on the shoulder. "Thanks. Let me know if anything comes up. I'm heading back to my office to...I don't know, plan some more. Make sure you keep anyone out unless they're delivering something."

"Of course, sir." The security guard turned back toward the front door.

Lyle walked past the empty front desk. At some point, he'd need to get a secretary, but he was still unsure if his puppets could perform very complicated tasks. As his experiments with the guard the last few days had proven, it was far too easy for a puppet to take his commands too literally.

It wouldn't be any fun to have an army of servants he needed to instruct about everything. A god needed proper worshippers, not puppets who didn't care about what they were doing.

Maybe I just need to hire a few people. If they work for me for a while and see how impressive I am, they'll start worshipping me, and other people will, too.

Lyle stepped into the hallway and headed toward his new office. It'd probably be temporary, as he imagined someone would eventually look into why the insurance adjusters in the office had all disappeared and stopped paying their bills, but the few deliveries so far had been easy enough to handle.

Doesn't everyone hate insurance companies anyway? Won't that slow things down? Maybe I should take over a lawyer's office next.

Lyle opened the door and moved to the chair behind the massive mahogany desk. He sat down and folded his hands in front of him. Thanks to Sarkazian's funds transfer, Lyle now had millions of dollars to play around with. As long as he was careful, he could use that to legitimately buy his own building and hire staff he didn't have to personally control, but there was one small problem.

The man frowned and brought up a web browser. He had the smarts and ambition, but he didn't have a decent plan. Wasting his power on something petty would be pointless. No, if he wanted to be a god, he needed to start doing things worthy of a god, or at least someone powerful.

Is this what they call a failure of imagination?

Conquering the underworld seemed like one possibility, but that'd place him in contact with not just common gangsters but dangerous magical beings who might anticipate his abilities and be more resistant. Simple, easy fraud through mind-control seemed a profitable if boring bet.

Lyle decided he needed a few billion dollars. After a few billion dollars, buying influence would be trivial.

If I end up the richest man in the world, everyone will treat me as a god. Then I can hire whoever I want, and people won't even question it. This is the perfect plan. I can't see how it could possibly go wrong.

The only thing Lyle was sure of was he needed to collect a few additional puppets immediately. As disappointing as his lack of current worshippers was, managing staff was still something he didn't know how to do well. But in the short-term, he needed to ensure he was protected.

A close encounter with a car the previous night had made it clear that he had to see a threat coming to deal with it. While the incident had revolved around a potential car accident, the next time it might be a PDA agent. A few bodyguards would help with that.

Now the age-old question: quantity or quality? Better double-check to see if anyone's looking for me. Don't want to go out and get knocked out by some lucky cop, but a few extras might be helpful to keep cops off my ass when the time comes.

Lyle tapped **LOS ANGELES EXPLOSION** into his browser and clicked on the first link returned. A video on a local news site auto-played.

A square-jawed, dark-haired reporter stood in front of a massive crater with a serious look on his face. Men and women in FBI jackets and suited witches and wizards in PDA jackets, their wands out, combed the crater.

The chyron below read, **PDA and FBI still investigating unexplained magical explosion in Sherman Oaks**.

"This is going to work out better than I hoped," Lyle murmured.

"The investigation continues into the recent unexplained explosion that was responsible for the confirmed death of at least fourteen people and the injury of eighteen others in Sherman Oaks," the reporter explained. "At this time, the PDA has confirmed that the explosion was magical in nature and centered on the crater you see behind me, where previously a large luxury home stood. The owner of the home, businessman John Sarkazian, is currently unaccounted for and is believed to have been killed in the explosion. Due to the high level of magical background residue, the PDA is having trouble isolating the number of victims at this location, given all the other injuries and deaths in the nearby homes."

The camera panned to the side to reveal several scorched houses, walls and roofs blown off.

"I am so impressive." Lyle clapped and grinned. He never got tired of seeing the destruction he'd wrought.

After the camera returned to the reporter, he nodded in the direction of a nearby PDA witch who crouched near the edge of the crater, her glowing wand cycling through different colors and her face pinched in concentration.

"Although the PDA personnel are being tightlipped, an anonymous source has informed me that this explosion was likely the result of a highly dangerous and illegal magical item called an 'elemental fusion crystal.' The question of why one or more of these crystals would be present in this home remains open to investigation. The authorities are asking anyone who has any information about this incident to contact the local FBI. However, the authorities have made clear that they do not believe this incident represents a continuing threat to the public at large."

Lyle leaned back in his chair with a huge smile on his face. He wasn't sure how much the PDA would figure out, but it sounded like he was in the clear. After all, they'd have no reason to suspect someone like him. That was one advantage of coming into power only recently.

"I'm getting away with so much, and I didn't even have to do much except flatten a neighborhood." Lyle rubbed his hands together in excitement. "I really *am* a god."

Complicated schemes involving controlling the mayor or chief of police would be the most practical, but they didn't seem as fun. What was the point of being a god if you had to hide half the time?

Lyle sighed, his dreams crashing back to Earth in the shadow of practical details. He needed more money, more influence, and more power, and once he had that, LA would become the seat of his new kingdom.

No one's going to be able to stop me because they don't even know about me.

Shay yawned as she slipped into bed. James was already in bed on the other side reading a news article on his phone about the big explosion. His brow was furrowed and his eyes were moving back and forth.

"They find out anything new yet on that?" Shay set the alarm on her phone and laid it on the nightstand. "Definitely wasn't a gas explosion. I can't even believe they were suggesting it might be."

"PDA confirmed it was those crystals." James grunted. "The FBI is now saying they think Sarkazian might have been a member of New Veil."

Shay snorted. "That's some poetic justice, then. If he was one of those assholes, he was probably messing around with some crap he shouldn't have and blew his ass up. The only shitty part is that he took innocent people with him. Fucking terrorist nut-jobs."

James nodded. "I was wondering if this shit would lead to some big local bounty, but you're right. It just sounds like some assholes who should have been more careful. No one's left to hunt down since they're all smears in that crater."

"Big bounty?" Shay peered at him. "Oh, you wanted a level five to round out the summer?"

"It's not a big deal. I'm not doing any special shit after

the summer, so I can always take on bounties." James shrugged. "It's not about that."

"Then what *is* it about?"

"Kicking those dust-dealers' asses the other day was fun, but Whispy's right. I need tougher enemies if I'm gonna get stronger. I need challenges for him and me."

"Huh?" Shay blinked. "Since when do you care what that whiny-ass killing machine has to say? You could be throwing asteroids at guys and he'd still be bitching about you getting stronger."

James set his phone down. "I thought all this shit would be over when I dealt with that crazy alien bitch, but then her buddy showed up. I probably could have taken them out if I had gone into extended advanced mode, but they'd probably just send another guy or multiple ships. He likely wasn't wrong when he said he could kill me by bombing me."

"So what? Johnston did his thing, and now they're leaving you alone. There's no reason to trust the government, but I think they don't want to let aliens do whatever the fuck they want either."

James frowned. "Wait, I thought you were the one telling me not to trust the government?"

Shay nodded. "Yeah, I don't think you should trust the government not to screw with you, but I think they'll actually keep the Alliance off you for their own reasons. Don't trust them. Use them."

"I'm protected for now." James frowned. "And how long will that last? Those fuckers think I'm a dangerous nuke that needs to taken out. How long will they stay away from me just because Johnston threatened them?"

Shay laughed. "You make him sound like he's just some local mobster. The guy's a senator, and you had a senator saying the country, and others, might toss nukes at the Alliance. You have to understand, James...it's not that I think you should trust the government. That'd be stupid. But you *do* have to trust that the government is wetting their pants about the idea of the Alliance thinking they can show up and do whatever the fuck they want."

"Yeah, for now, but what if the government decides I'm more trouble than I'm worth?" James' hands curled into fists. "I'm not gonna let anyone fuck with me, but it's like we talked about before. I'm not gonna fight the Army."

"We'll figure something out. Peyton and Heather are keeping an eye on things, so at the minimum, we won't be surprised, but to be honest, I'm pretty sure the government knows not to screw with you." Shay pointed to the amulet lying on his nightstand. "And as long as you have that, I think that's gonna continue, whether or not they understand everything about it."

James leaned over and picked up the amulet. "There's also some other shit I wonder about. I wasn't thinking about it much until recently when Alison was talking about the portals class she has at school."

"What?"

"I went to Oriceran from my home planet through a long-range portal." James set the amulet back down. "Everything that the alien bitch said made it sound like my people use only portals, not ships."

Shay nodded. "What does that have to do with anything?"

James glared at the amulet. "I'm supposed to call the others, right? The other Vax?"

"Yeah, but you're not going to." Shay shrugged. "And obviously Whispy can't do it himself, or he already would have."

"Think it through. The Nine Systems assholes are obsessed with me doing it, but there's another way this could go down."

"I don't understand."

James looked over at her. "What do you think the government would do if they lost a nuke tomorrow?"

Shay winced. "Go look for it."

"Exactly." James narrowed his eyes.

"But you've been on Earth for over thirty years. If the Vax gave a shit, why not come already?"

"Maybe they're still looking. It's a big damned galaxy. Even with those recovered memories, I don't understand everything that happened when my parents sent me away. But if you could open a portal once, why couldn't you do it again?"

"That's why you're concerned about getting stronger?" Shay replied.

"I know that little shit has the potential to call them, but I've got him under control. But what would happen if they showed up tomorrow?" James stared into the distance. "Extended advanced mode is pretty badass, but I don't think it would be enough. If the Vax can conquer planets, they've got more firepower than what I've used so far, which means Whispy's right. I need to find tougher guys; guys who'll push me to my limit, until the point where I'm not sure I can win. I need to become a Forerunner."

Shay laid her head on her pillow. "They might never come, James. You can't spend your whole life waiting for an alien invasion. And even if they do come, you're just one man. Yes, one very badass man, but I'm sure the military could handle it."

"That Nine Systems douchebag was ready to drop an antimatter torpedo on me, he was so scared. I don't think a few Marines in exoskeletons will cut it."

Shay snorted. "Then nukes, or strategic-level magic. It's not your damned responsibility to protect the entire world. You're a bounty hunter. Go after bounties, or help me out on tomb raids, but you're not the Army. Let the guys in fancy uniforms worry about an alien invasion."

"I just want to make sure I clean up my own shit." James rested his head in his linked hands on the pillow. "That's the one thing I keep thinking about. How maybe I should be going around and taking down level fives or sixes wherever I can find them."

Shay scoffed. "We don't know if that'd be helpful, and trust me, there's not going to be a nice barbeque place everywhere you go. If you care so much, maybe you can come with me on my next tomb raid. I'm sure there will be something annoying and challenging. Smite-Williams contacted Peyton and wants to meet with me tomorrow to discuss it."

"I'm going to that musical with Alison tomorrow." James grunted. "I promised her, and it's the last big thing I'm doing with her before she goes back to school."

"It's fine." Shay turned to smile at him. "It's not like I need you there for the briefing. If it's something Whispy can have a little fun on, I'll bring you along. If I don't need you, I won't."

"What about Lily?"

Shay narrowed her eyes. "She's still looking into that thing in Trinidad."

James glanced at Shay. "You sure she's not just taking a little vacation?"

Shay grinned. "Maybe, but she's earned it. And Alison's not the only one running out of summer. I do want to get in one last job. If it's a good job, you can come along, kill some evil wizard or some shit, and get closer to growing a super-cannon or whatever when you're pissed. Maybe by the time we get back to LA, there will be a rampaging army of Drow for you to cut through."

"That might be fun."

"That might be fun?" Shay snickered. "Enjoy your show with Alison tomorrow."

James made a face. "I enjoy spending time with her. Not gonna enjoy the show."

Shay stared at him. "So you're a man who looks forward to fighting an entire warehouse filled with criminals, but you worry about a musical?"

James sighed. "The fucking criminals didn't sing at me."

CHAPTER NINE

Shay frowned as she sat down across from the Professor at the Leanan Sidhe. His reddened face suggested that Father O'Banion had already come out to play, which didn't speak well for having a decent meeting about tomb raiding opportunities. Even Smite-Williams had his limits.

Come on. You were the one who told me to come, and you end up drunk off your ass before I even show up? That's bullshit.

The Professor held up a half-empty frosted mug. "A very good afternoon to you, Miz Carson. I haven't seen you in a couple of months. I miss the light your beauty shines on my day."

"Damn, you really are drunk." Shay realized a few seconds later her back was to the door.

Shit. Does it even matter? If I'm gonna get taken out, it probably won't be in this place. I don't know all the tricks Smite-Williams has set up here, but I get the feeling it'd be a sad fucking day if anyone ever went after the Leanan Sidhe, and that's not even taking into account what James might do.

"Your assistant was overly eager," the Professor explained. "Which suggests that *you're* overly eager. I'm not one to tell you your business, but desperation doesn't make for a good position in a negotiation. Something to keep in mind."

Shay snorted. "You're not gonna start fucking me over now after working together for years, especially when I'm marrying James. You're not the kind of guy who likes to screw over people in negotiations anyway."

The Professor chuckled. "Aye, that's true. But why the sudden interest in a high-end job? I've not heard anything to suggest either you or James would need an infusion of cash." He eyed her. "Unless you're trying to get him to buy you a large island or something for the wedding. You don't seem the type, I must admit."

"It's nothing like that." Shay shrugged. "Just wanted to go out on a good job before I take a few months off is all. I wanted a job that would actually challenge me and keep me satisfied for a few months until the next big job."

"I see. That makes perfect sense. In that case…" The Professor gulped down some beer. "Cursed cobza."

"Huh?" Shay blinked. "How drunk *are* you? You're just stringing words together now. This is a serious request, Smite-Williams. I'm not here to play around with Father O'Banion. You told Peyton you had something, which was why I bothered to come."

The older man laughed and shook his head. "No, no. A *cobza*. It's a stringed instrument used in folk music, particularly Hungarian and Romanian folk music. It's kind of like a lute."

Shay blinked. "Okay, so you weren't just stringing words together. You're talking about an instrument?

"Aye."

"You want me to find a cursed instrument?"

The Professor set his mug down. "I supposed 'cursed' is a bit misleading, since it's not cursed in the traditional sense that it creates a negative situation for the user. It works completely as intended, which makes it more an incredibly dangerous magical instrument rather than a cursed artifact."

Shay frowned. "And what does this *cobza* do, exactly? Blow shit up? Turn people into stone or weird statues?"

"If only it were so straightforward." The Professor's smile dimmed but didn't disappear. "It drives listeners insane when played the appropriate way and fed the necessary magical energy to sustain the inherent spell, and with the help of a little amplification, it could easily drive tens of thousands into madness, if not more."

"Does this shit work if you hear the music over the radio or on a recording?"

"I'm not entirely sure." The Professor offered her a sheepish smile. "Unfortunately, or fortunately, depending on how you look at it, the last time it was used was in a village that lacked any such technology in the early 20th century. At that time, though, it resulted in a lethal riot that killed over half the people in the village, and it's been associated with several other dangerous incidents in Romanian history. It's usually only limited location that has prevented it from creating worse disasters."

Huh. I did ask for a major job, and this sounds like one.

Shay shook her head. "I don't get it. Who makes an

instrument that drives people nuts? What good is that? They're just doing something for evil shits and giggles?"

"It's less evil for amusement's sake and more for revenge if the stories are to be believed. I'm not a hundred percent certain, but my research suggests its origins lie in a musician wizard whose wife caught the eye of a corrupt nobleman." The Professor took another drink. "The woman was dragged off to be the nobleman's plaything, and when the musician tried to recover her, he was beaten within an inch of his life, and he found out shortly after that his wife had committed suicide."

Shay grimaced. "Shit, that's depressing, but I suppose I shouldn't have expected that a legend about a cobza of madness was going to be full of sweetness and light."

"Indeed. The legend states that upon learning what happened, the musician flew into a rage and sold his soul to the Devil in exchange for vengeance. He crafted the instrument and imbued it with its strange and deadly power before inciting madness in the castle of the nobleman who'd taken his wife. The musician blamed everyone inside for failing to save her."

"Is it true?"

The Professor shrugged. "There was an unexplained historical episode of deadly mass insanity in the Banat region that might be related. Historians previously attributed it to ergot poisoning, but it's like many incidents of the past, in that it needs to be re-examined in the context of Oriceran." He sighed. "It's hard to ignore that there might be a deeper truth. I'm dubious it's the result of an infernal pact as opposed to basic applied magic, but we've both seen many odd and bizarrely evil things in our careers so I won't say it's impossible."

Every lecture Shay gave at UCLA reinforced that concept. She was the last person to ever question if magic might have been involved in an incident, and if not magic, perhaps non-Oriceran aliens. The truth of Oriceran's existence didn't clear up every single mystery for humanity. In many cases, it had created new ones.

"That shit sounds like bad news," Shay observed. "Any random terrorist or dictator could play his way to a slaughter, and if it works over the radio or internet?" She shuddered.

The Professor shook his head. "This is one time where at least the world has smiled at us, at least in a small way. As I noted, it requires that magic be fed into it, which means a magical of some sort needs to be the one using it. Now, this wouldn't preclude a wizard or Oriceran helping some random terrorist or dictator, as you point out, but at least it's not something any random person can use. That said, dark wizard factions have been increasing their activities in recent years, so it's best to be careful—which is why I'm so keen on its quick recovery. We don't want to give them any opportunities."

"Yeah, not exactly the kind of thing anyone wants lying around." Shay paused as a waitress came by to pick up the Professor's mug and hand him a new one. She looked at Shay expectantly, and Shay waved her off. "I'm good, thanks."

The waitress departed, carefully weaving through the dense crowd that filled the pub.

Shay turned back to the Professor. "You said it hasn't

been used since the beginning of the last century?"

"Around there, yes." The Professor furrowed his brow and nodded a second later.

"So it's been lost since then?"

The Professor nodded. "Aye. It was in fact completely lost until last week, when I became aware through my sources that an unscrupulous sort had recovered it in Romania and was intending to smuggle it from there to the UK, and then who knows where?"

"Okay, that sounds promising. You don't mind if I take it from this other asshole then, right?" Shay gave him a questioning look. "Not saying I'm going to kill the guy, but not gonna go out of my way to let him kill me when I grab the cobza."

"That won't be necessary." The Professor offered her a bright smile. "Romania has already done that for you. You have no direct competition, or at least not yet."

"He was executed by the government? Convenient." Shay leaned back. "I don't mind doing the whole 'woman versus environment' thing rather than 'woman versus man.'"

"No, no. Not *that* government. The smuggler involved decided he was going to evade certain authorities by hiding in the Hoia Baciu Forest. Have you heard of it?"

Shay scratched her cheek. "It sounds familiar, but I can't quite place it."

"It's a forest in Transylvania," the Professor explained. "It's had a haunted reputation for quite some time, but before the gates opened, there was just the occasional sighting and that sort of thing. There was nothing particularly sinister."

"And now that the gates are open? I'm guessing it's a lot more sinister?"

It wouldn't be the first place she'd traveled to with that problem. While most people treated the opening of the gates as just having a few witches, elves, and gnomes running around in public, it'd already resulted in many changes on Earth.

The Professor nodded gravely. "The level of magic in the forest ended up being far higher than many other places; even most kemanas. It's my understanding that in the distant past, it was an area where certain dangerous experiments with portal and gate magic were performed. Several sources blame the Atlanteans, but they might have been painted as the culprits out of convenience. The truth is that the place is permanently damaged, in a sense, with fluctuating levels of magic, and even random portals opening on occasion."

"I see," Shay replied, taking in all the information. The more she could learn about the job, the less trouble she'd have completing it.

He gave a slight shrug. "Previously, the Silver Griffins and certain wizards associated with the Romanian government did their best to keep an eye on it without drawing more attention to it by trying to keep people out. It's gotten steadily worse since the gates opened, and now it's completely out of hand. Although the Griffins were destroyed, no one has a problem simply informing people that the place is too dangerous for most to travel to. That's helped keep people safe, even though the underlying problem hasn't been dealt with."

Shay leaned forward. "Break down what you mean by

'it's completely out of hand.' I don't know if I like the sound of that."

"Many different things. Strange portals open at random. The place is also infested with dangerous magical creatures that don't seem to care or even know what century it is. Electromagnetic interference makes most technology people try to use in it fail. It's so bad that the Romanian government has closed off the entire area, and they have the military patrolling the perimeter to keep people out and the creatures in. They're looking into ways to stabilize it because it's feared that any attacks on the area might result in an even worse situation. The Veil is thin in many places in the world, but usually only on particular days, not all the time."

Shay chuckled. "Damn, when I wanted a big job, I wasn't thinking you were going to send me into hell. I have to admit it sounds fun!"

"Oh, it's not hell. Or, none of the creatures are demons, anyway." The Professor waggled his eyebrows. "But, aye, Miz Carson, it's extremely dangerous. As such, I'd suggest James accompany you on this job. You might be able to handle all the threats, but it wouldn't hurt to have a strong backup."

"I was planning to ask him anyway. He's been looking for a major ass-kicking opportunity." Shay smiled. "And this sounds right up his alley. My only question is, how the hell do I find some instrument in the middle of a whacked-out forest filled with dangerous monsters."

The Professor laughed. "The Fixer gave me an artifact that will help on this particular job."

"What's so funny about that?"

"It's ridiculous-looking. You'll see. It's a little chicken figurine with a rotating base. He's attuned it to track the cobza."

Shay blinked. "Not to be a bitch… Who am I kidding, I *am* just being a bitch. Why isn't he going and grabbing it himself?"

The Professor smirked. "He's currently involved in other important matters. You do have to keep in mind, Miz Carson, that the Fixer is responsible for the entire planet, and there are a lot of dangerous things going on all the time on Earth."

Shay pulled out her phone to tap in a quick text to Peyton. "This sounds like a good job. When did you need it done?"

"Sooner rather than later."

Shay frowned and nodded. "Could you give me a few days? I think I'll need them to get James onboard."

The Professor nodded. "That's fine."

"By the way, you said the military is patrolling the forest. Do you know of any places that are weaker in the perimeter? I'd rather not have a shootout with a bunch of soldiers."

The Professor pulled out his own phone and sent her some information. "Don't worry. I have some contacts there who will be able to get you past the patrols, but of course, those military forces won't come and help you if you're in trouble. You'll be on your own."

"Fine. The only things worth being afraid of in that forest will be James and me." Shay grinned.

CHAPTER TEN

Trey relaxed in a corner booth at the White Sun, just soaking in the light jazz playing over the speakers. He was taking his time as he sipped his Manhattan and checking out everybody in the room. Although he was now full-time in Vegas, he still couldn't identify every major criminal on sight, and that was a hole in his knowledge he needed to correct to provide the best leadership for the local Brownstone Agency.

The more I know, the less I'll be surprised.

Kathy chatted quietly with a man at the bar, laughing with her hand on his arm. Trey was always impressed by the differences in how she and Tyler operated, but they both got useful information in the end. He respected them both for that. Even James had to rely on information brokers for his job, proving how critical they were to a good bounty hunter.

I might never be as great at this job as the big man, but there's no reason I can't get close.

A suited man with slick-backed hair entered the White

Sun and looked around. Trey recognized the new arrival. He was Marco Esposito, a local man; son of the leader of the Esposito Family.

Well, look what we have here.

The bounty hunter didn't bother to hide his frown. He hadn't had any trouble with the Mafia in a few months, but his last few major dealings with them hadn't left him with much trust in their ability not to stir up trouble. Plus, every once in a while, one of their guys gave him a dirty look or made some annoying comment that reminded him they weren't on good terms.

I hope those fuckers have learned their lesson. I'm already tired of dealing with their shit. If they come at me again, maybe I won't be so nice next time.

The mobster continued scanning the room until his gaze landed on the bounty hunter. A slight smile followed as he walked toward Trey, his stride easy and loose. He didn't look like he was preparing for a fight.

This is promising shit.

Trey sighed and shook his head, unsure. If Esposito started any trouble in the White Sun, Trey would need to make an example of him, if only to make sure that everyone knew that just because the big man wasn't there, that didn't mean they could push the Brownstone Agency around. The value of the place as an information source would go down if people didn't believe the neutrality would be defended, too.

Esposito stopped beside the booth and offered Trey a pleasant smile. The man had blindingly white teeth.

Damn. He must use those to light up the road at night.

"Mr. Garfield. We haven't met, but I'm Marco Esposito." He extended his hand.

"I know who you are." Trey narrowed his eyes and gave the other man's hand a light shake. "The only real question is why the fuck you are here and talking to me? I guess that's two questions."

The mobster chuckled. "I like you. None of this fake politeness bullshit. No wonder you work for Brownstone." He nodded at the seat opposite Trey. "I'd like to join you to discuss certain matters. I think you'll find this interesting to listen to and at least think about. But I wouldn't want to impose."

Trey's gaze flicked around the room. There were a few other men from various Families and factions present, but none seemed to be paying him or Esposito particular attention. If this was some sort of trap, it wasn't obvious, and the meeting wasn't considered noteworthy enough by others to require close personal scrutiny.

"I don't mind talking to any man who just wants to drink with me," Trey replied evenly.

"Good." Esposito sat and folded his hands in front of him. "First off, let me note that I'm aware that you've had some unpleasant dealings with some of the local Family men. Obviously, each of our groups has its own concerns and goals, but everyone now mutually agrees that it was a mistake to antagonize you—and our Families don't always agree on things." He chuckled.

Trey snorted. "You're damned right it was a mistake. So, what, you here to apologize and shit? Kind of took a long time, don't you think?"

Not gonna be petty, but also can't let them think I'm too "live and let lie."

"While I do apologize, that's not why I'm here." Esposito smiled. "I'm here instead to talk about mutually beneficial opportunities, things would benefit both you and us. In the end, we're both businessmen, right? So that's what we should be focusing on: business."

Trey furrowed his brow. "Opportunities? What opportunities?"

"Yes. You see, we Family men understand and respect strength. We also understand and respect people who keep their word. Say what you will about Brownstone and his agency, no one's ever said that James Brownstone doesn't keep his word, even if it involves him saying he's going to fuck someone up."

Trey chuckled. "Yeah, that's the big man, and that's how we run things. We ain't going around looking for fights to start. We just go after people who already have made a big enough mess to get themselves a bounty."

Esposito leaned forward, a plastic smile on his face. "That's the thing. Your agency is still new in town, and I get it—you've got money to make. We could help with that."

Trey frowned. "You could help us with that? How? We don't need leads. We go after public bounties."

The other man's smile never wavered. "I understand that, but we could provide you with opportunities and point you at certain people making things unpleasant for people of concern here in the fine city of Las Vegas. For example, we might be able to highlight where certain bounties might be when you otherwise have trouble finding them. You take them down and get your money, and people concerned with local stability benefit. That's not objectionable, now, is it?"

Trey snorted. "What? Let me get this straight. Are you saying the Brownstone Agency should form some sort of motherfucking alliance with the Vegas Mafia?"

Esposito sighed. "I'm just saying that we both represent businesses interested in making money. You people are bounty hunters, not cops, so perhaps certain accommodations could be made that would be mutually beneficial to all parties, especially in terms of taking certain rewards to perhaps focus on not every available bounty. A short-term loss for a long-term profit is a valid business strategy."

Oh, hell *no. Is he saying what I think he's saying? Time to set some shit straight.*

"You said your name is Marco Esposito?" Trey asked.

"Yes, and call me Marco. All my friends do."

We ain't friends yet, bitch, but I'll play nice so you'll listen to what I have to say.

Trey cleared his throat. "Let me break it down for you then, Marco. I was under the impression already that everyone local understood how this shit worked, and I'm kind of frustrated that I have to explain it again, especially for someone who seems like he's a pretty smart guy."

Marco shrugged. "Go ahead, break it down for me. This ought to be interesting." He looked more curious than annoyed.

"It ain't no thing. It's like you said. We ain't 5-0. We're bounty hunters, but that's the thing. Because we're bounty hunters, we go after anyone with a bounty, because anyone with a bounty has already fucked up enough and made enough noise that they need to be handled directly." Trey picked up his drink and took a sip. "And once we're committed to going after a bounty, we ain't gonna take money to look the other way just because you're Mafia, if that's what you were getting at. The minute the Brownstone Agency does that shit, it looks like we're taking sides, and that causes all sorts of problems. You know what I'm saying?"

Marco frowned, the first significant displeasure he'd shown since starting the conversation. "I think you're pushing away some very good opportunities for us to be friends. I believe you will want to think about this very carefully, or perhaps bring it up with Mr. Brownstone."

Trey laughed. "You're tripping if you think that James Brownstone is gonna take bribes to ignore a bounty, and he's told me a shitload of times that I can run Vegas however I need to."

"I see." Marco's mouth twitched. "That's unfortunate."

Trey sighed. "Let me make this shit clear. I may have knocked some heads around, and some local people learned why they shouldn't fuck with me, but I ain't shit compared to James Brownstone. Hell, that was why other fuckers came after me, and if this shit is about threatening me, well, learn your damned lesson, bitches. Even if you manage to push *me* aside, you're not gonna want to deal with the big man." He gestured toward the door.

The mobster quickly recovered his smile. "Let me give you a scenario, Mr. Garfield, so I can make sure we're both on the same page. I think we can still reach an accommodation that's mutually beneficial as long as each party understands the other."

"Fine. Go ahead." Trey leaned back and crossed his arms.

"You're not a cop. Neither is your boss." Marco glanced over at a single uniformed officer on the far end of the bar. "So it is our understanding, which has only been reinforced by this conversation, that if a Family man hasn't threatened you and doesn't have a bounty, you wouldn't have any interest in them. Is that an accurate statement of the situation?"

Trey lifted his chin and gave a slight nod. "Yeah, that's true. You keep your shit clean in public and avoid bounties, and you won't have a Brownstone problem unless you go looking for one. We've got better shit to do than run around messing with every fucker out there."

"And the Harriken? Everyone says James Brownstone didn't used to care about those sorts of groups, and although there was an organizational bounty when he finally took them down, initially there were mostly only low-level bounties."

"Because they disrespected the big man, and I'd think y'all would understand." Trey laughed. "Those Harriken bitches were the dumbest motherfuckers on the planet. He would have left their asses alone after the first time if they hadn't come at him again."

"I see." A combination of concern and slight confusion played out over Marco's face.

"Here's the deal." Trey picked up his drink and took a sip. "You know what the big man wants out of life?"

Marco furrowed his brow. "A lot of money, I'd assume. That's where we can help him."

"Shit, no. He don't give a fuck about that. If you had seen his house, you'd be asking yourself, 'How does a mother-fucker who has that much money live in some tiny house in the middle of a shitty neighborhood?" Trey held up a hand. "And I know it is a shitty neighborhood because that's where I was born and raised and lived most of my life. Sure, the place is now getting better, but that's just the last year or so."

"I don't get it. If he doesn't care about money, what *does* he care about? He's not a justice freak, or he wouldn't be so obsessed with only going after bounties. What? Are you saying Brownstone doesn't care about shit except for the thrill of the hunt?" Marco sat up with a disturbed look on his face.

Oh, so you fuckers thought you had him all worked out, is that it?

Trey almost laughed in his face. The idea of playing James up as some ruthless coldblooded hunter appealed, but keeping the Vegas situation reasonable and stable was at the top of his list of concerns. He wasn't about to sign some treaty with the Mafia, but if he could keep them on their best behavior, it'd make things better for both the agency and the cops. It was just a matter of managing expectations on both sides.

"Nah, you still ain't getting it." Trey shook his head. "The big man wants a simple life, but he's got a talent for ass-kicking, so he ended up a bounty hunter. Now shit's no longer simple for him, so whenever anyone can make something easier and simpler, it makes him less cranky and less likely to throw said motherfucker through a window. You know what I'm saying?"

Marco nodded slowly, some of the fear retreating from

his face and the smarm seeping back in. "I think a lot of people are like that. It's understandable."

Trey stared at him for a few seconds. "Exactly. So, nah, the Brownstone Agency don't want no special shit from you, other than what you feel like giving, and you shouldn't expect no special shit from us other than you keep your guys away from bounties and away from us and we won't have no problems. Is that clear enough for you, Marco?"

"I appreciate your candor, Mr. Garfield."

"You can call me Trey."

"Okay, Trey." Marco smiled. "We Family men are still figuring out how we feel about the changes in Vegas over the last couple of years. The Brownstone Agency moving into town has made things interesting. Me personally? I kind of like it."

Trey chuckled. "You like it? Color me skeptical, Marco. I don't see how anyone who does something on a certain side of the law would like the fact that there was a bounty hunter like Brownstone in town."

"I understand why you might think I'm spouting bull-shit, but the truth is that the agency being here makes things fresh in a way they haven't been in a while. Probably not since the gates opened." Marco's gaze flicked to an elf in the corner.

"We have an understanding, then?" Trey stared at him. "I don't want any misunderstandings. I only want mother-fucking trouble from people I'm looking for mother-fucking trouble from, and you seem like a reasonable enough guy, Marco."

"Yes, I think we have an understanding." Marco pushed himself up as the waitress arrived. "And I'll let everyone else know, but I can't vouch for every group in the city. Please keep that in mind if there are any more incidents?"

Trey frowned. "Do you expect there to be more incidents?"

"Not offhand, but this *is* Las Vegas. It's always best to expect the unexpected."

"Fair enough."

Marco nodded to Trey and walked away.

The waitress looked at the bounty hunter and he shook his head.

What does that shit mean? Does that mean they ain't gonna fuck with us going forward? Or just some of them? Suppose we won't really know until we grab someone they give a shit about.

Trey lifted his glass and snorted. "Interesting is just another way of saying complicated."

CHAPTER ELEVEN

James glanced at Shay before he turned the corner in the F-350. She was talking to Peyton on the phone as they made their way to a florist. While James didn't care much about whatever flowers they might have at the wedding, Shay insisted it wouldn't hurt for him to come along and note anything he might have absolute and unyielding objections to. She also admitted she wasn't sure *she* cared about having flowers at the wedding, and even suggested they get Zoe to find them some Oriceran fighting plants guests could battle for fun at the reception.

Shit. Now that I think of it, that doesn't sound half-bad. I wonder if she was joking?

"Uh-huh." Shay nodded. "Thanks, Peyton. No, I think it's a good time to do that, especially given how the timing of everything else is going to work out. Okay, I'll talk to you later." She ended the call and slipped her phone back into her pocket.

"You sure about that?" James asked. "From what I heard in the first half, it sounded like you were telling him to go on a vacation. You really want him to go away right before you head out on a major tomb raid?"

"Heather's on a three-week vacation right now, so why not Peyton?" Shay shrugged.

James slowed as they approached a light. "I just wanted to give her some time. I've fucked her over on vacations before, and since high-level shit was slow and she had to do all those background checks, she deserved time off."

"Peyton's been whining about going on vacation with his girlfriend for a while," Shay explained. "And from what the Professor said, having a remote hacker on this job will be worthless anyway. Good time for everyone to get in their summer fun. Otherwise, it's just him sitting around being bored while I'm kicking ass and out of communication."

James shrugged and stopped at a red light. "We can't leave until Alison's back on the train, so not for another forty-eight hours."

"That's fine. The Professor wanted it handled within a week according to his follow-up message, but he was flexible about schedule other than that. The Fixer's stupid figurine should take us right to it. I swear that he's just fucking with me, or maybe he's fucking with the Professor."

James grunted. "Who gives a shit, as long as it works?"

"It's still annoying."

"And what about Lily? Check in with her? She might want in on this." James accelerated as the light changed. "Or is she still in Trinidad?"

Shay nodded. "Yeah. She admitted she is on vacation, and Harry just flew down there yesterday, so she's going to be distracted for a little longer. I don't give a shit. She's done plenty of jobs, and it's good that she can take on some of these easier jobs by herself. She might as well have a little vacation, too."

James grunted. "So this is like a date trip for us, then?"

He wasn't sure if that was a good thing. He was more interested in pushing his adaptation to the limit. Even a few surprise nanoforms would be welcome.

Shay frowned and shook her head. "Nope, not at all."

"Why's that?"

"I'm not that worried, but this shit also doesn't sound simple. I've been studying more about the forest, and it's a fucked-up place. It's no wonder the Romanian government just sealed the entire place up. Some of the creatures that have been spotted there haven't been reported for centuries anywhere else, and that's assuming we don't fall through some sort of portal. We're going to have to be damned careful while we're there. We don't know what could attack us, and what kind of tactics they might use."

"Good," James rumbled. "That's the kind of workout I want. It's a good time, too. I just checked the bounty app, and there's nothing that even looks like a possible level four heading toward LA or Vegas."

"What about the New Veil shit?"

James shook his head. "I asked Maria to check with the AET and see if they heard anything, and from what she said, the government thinks it's over; a bunch of terrorists played with something they shouldn't have and are dead. They are looking for one person of interest, but they don't think he has any of the crystals. The PDA did some sort of magical tracing thing to confirm it."

I wonder if Whispy could have protected me from an explo-

sion like that? I doubt the PDA will let me bring over some of those crystals to test it out. Would Shay let me?

Of course, she would. She had too much fun trying to fuck me up when she first realized Whispy was adaptive.

"Huh." Shay nodded. "So, we should be good to go to Romania and find the Professor's evil instrument for him once Alison heads back to school."

"Yeah," James replied. He furrowed his brow. "Are there vampires there? We're not just going to fucking Romania; we're going to Transylvania. I know a lot of that shit is just from the book, but there were legends even before the book."

"That's the weird thing." Shay chuckled and shook her head. "Werewolves in the form of shifters are all too real. We've got wizards and witches and all sorts of weird regional monsters, but the Stoker aristocratic vampire-type creature, as far as I know, doesn't actually exist, and never has."

James grunted in genuine surprise. "You're shitting me? There are no vampires in Romania? I always figured there weren't any over here, but they all still lived in the Old Country. Kind of like you ran into those weird-ass frog guys only in Russia, even if you can find gnomes and elves everywhere."

"I've looked into this a lot." Shay waved her hand. "I checked out a lot of sources, old and new. There are creatures out there that feed on blood, but most of them are obviously monstrous or bestial. They are nothing like the classic literary vampire, not even the tortured Nosferatu." She shrugged. "There doesn't seem to be, even with the gates open, a true vampire in the modern sense. No semi-intelligent human-looking person who subsists only on blood and doesn't eat flesh, too. There were reports in history of wizards with specific blood curses, and a lot of modern historians wonder if the legends got mixed up with those wizards to explain why we have this idea."

James grunted. "I don't give a shit if they live in a castle or like to fuck people. What about just corpses who like to drink blood and have magic powers?"

"Not outside things directly controlled by necromancers." Shay shook her head, obvious disbelief on her face. "It's weird. If there *is* anything like vampires, they've been very good at hiding."

"Turns out there are aliens." James shrugged. "Maybe there are vampires, too."

"Maybe. Stranger things have happened. Like *you*. Alien vampires?"

"That would be annoying as shit." James snorted. "If we won't be running into vampires, what will we be running into?"

"I don't know." Shay grimaced. "There are all sorts of local legends about different creatures, from dragons to flesh-eating ghouls. I think we should plan for basically everything and anything. It's time to give Whispy a real workout in an unusual magical area."

James turned another corner. It would be just a few more minutes until they arrived at the florist. "I'm kind of surprised the Professor thought you needed to go in and get the thing. If this forest is so fucked up and crawling with bullshit, the instrument's probably safe. It's not like some random hiker's gonna go in and grab it."

"Sure, safe from idiots like the Hollingsworth crew, but not from, say, something like the Council."

"They're all fucking dead. We killed them."

Shay nodded. "Sure, but there's always another asshole out there, and now we have two planets to provide our asshole supply."

James chuckled. "And we had plenty of assholes to begin with."

"Exactly."

"Not complaining. I'm hoping to get Whispy trained more. It's just hard to find shit he hasn't been exposed to. And I'm tough, but given the way the Alliance is wetting their pants about the Vax, I feel like I'm missing out on some shit. Even Whispy says I'm not at my maximum."

Shay frowned. "You can't trust that thing, remember? It's effectively an evil biocomputer that was supposed to take control of your mind. I know I was the one who encouraged you to use him, and I'm not saying you should *never* use him, but keep in mind what he wants and what you want are two separate things."

"Yeah, I get that. I don't trust Whispy, but I'm in control, so don't worry."

"Famous last words." Shay chuckled. "Big change from when I met you. I remember when you used to keep that thing locked up in your so-called warehouse."

James gave her a lopsided grin. "Some of us don't need five warehouses. One will do."

Shay rolled her eyes. "It was annoying as hell to go get it."

"I thought it was demonic before, and I didn't want it to

fall into the wrong hands," James replied. "Now I know it wouldn't have worked for anybody but Vax."

Shay laughed. "So since it's not infernal evil, you can tolerate it?"

"Something like that. At least my soul's not on the line." James changed lanes. The shopping center with the florist was coming up on their right.

Shay chuckled. "And it doesn't hurt to always be more prepared. The worst thing that happens is nothing."

James turned into the parking lot of the shopping center, the pink sign for the florist visible in the distance. "Hey, were you joking about the fighting plants?"

Shay blinked. "Huh? Yeah, I was." She laughed. "But now that you mention it, it's not a half-bad idea."

CHAPTER TWELVE

D*ad looks kind of worried*, Alison thought. *But he always kind of does, even when he's at Jessie Rae's.*

James pulled the F-350 into an open space in the Starbucks parking lot and put it in Park. "I'm gonna miss you, Alison. I hope your summer didn't totally suck. I tried to make sure to do more stuff you like this summer."

"You didn't have to do that, but I appreciated it." Alison unbuckled her seatbelt and leaned over to hug him. "It was a great summer, Dad." She smiled. "And we didn't have any annoying court cases or reporters this time. Even most of the bounties were fun."

James looked thoughtful "That's true. I didn't really think about that. That's a real good point."

"This was a great summer. It'll be hard to top it next year."

Alison sighed happily and patted his hand before opening the door. The myriad colors from the souls of everyone inside the Starbucks stood out in her internal darkness, along with the bright magic of the wall concealing the path to the magic train she'd be taking to a Starbucks in Charlottesville before heading back to the School of Necessary Magic.

She grabbed her small rolling suitcase from the back and stepped to the ground with practiced ease. She offered her father a happy smile. "Every time I talk to you and every time I come back, I'm happy, Dad. And I'm happy you're getting married. From the moment I met you, I could see in your soul that you were a good man, and you deserve this. I hope you realize that."

James grunted and looked away. "Have a nice trip back. Say hi to the *boy* for me."

Alison laughed. "I will, and I love you, Dad."

"I love you, too, Alison."

With a final wave, the teen closed the door and made her way into Starbucks, pulling her suitcase behind her. She didn't need a magical pulse to help her trace out the locations. The layout of the store was familiar, and she could easily extrapolate a path through it from the position of the soul energy of the various customers inside.

No one would question her small rolling suitcase since people were used to the occasional odd suitcase in Starbucks, even if few realized why an unusual number of magicals had them.

It's kind of weird that the train's still mostly a secret. I wonder when it'll be more known.

Alison stopped and turned around, watching her Dad's soul colors recede as he pulled out of the parking lot and then up the street. They were a bittersweet mix of happiness and sadness.

I've told him about Tanner, but not about a lot of the other stuff. I feel kind of bad about that. Waiting until I graduate is the best plan, though. He'd pull me out of the school if he knew all the crazy things that have been happening. Besides, it's not like anything that dangerous will happen again. There's only so much weird stuff that can happen at one school, even the School of Necessary Magic.

Bright anger flared from a man's soul as he stalked toward the counter. Alison wondered if they'd gotten his drink order wrong, but the fear that flowed a second later from around others and what she could see about the motion of his hand from the extension of his soul energy was familiar enough, if only from her bounties. She couldn't always make out the fine details, but in this case, she knew exactly what was happening.

Oh, no. He's got a gun.

"Give me what's in the register, bitch," the man screamed.

Some people edged toward the exit, while others rushed straight out. Some people screamed in surprise. The colors of fear, concern, and anger mixed together all over the room.

Alison stood firm as people brushed past her. She squared her shoulders and kept her attention on the robber and his soul energy, looking for any subtle shifts that might announce he was going to shoot. She'd had more than a little practice over the last two summers looking at the energy of dangerous criminals.

With shaking hands, the employee opened the register. Overwhelming shades of fear covered her soul. "There's only twenty in here. P-people a-almost always pay with their c-cards or p-phones now."

The man grabbed the woman. "I should fucking kill you, bitch. Fine, you're coming with me then, in case the cops come. I knew I should have hit the bank instead."

What would Dad do? He'd try to act like he didn't want to get involved, but then he'd kick ass.

Alison let go of her suitcase and layered an invisible shield using light magic over herself, then walked over to the man, her hands raised above her head. "Take me instead."

The color of confusion leaked into the anger and greed. "What?" the man barked.

"You need a hostage, right?" Alison smiled. "The police are less likely to shoot if it's a young girl." She nodded toward the employee. Given the woman's voice and soul textures, she was probably middle-aged.

The man laughed. "You stupid little bitch, you want to be a hero? This ain't no game."

"I'm just trying to give you an option."

"Fine," the man replied.

Alison couldn't see the gun, but she could tell he was pointing it at her as he demanded, "Turn around and put your hands on your fucking head."

She complied and sighed.

Nothing but hate and anger and greed in his soul. Most of the bounties we went after this summer had more beauty in their souls.

The employee collapsed to her knees and started sobbing, then scrambled into the back on her hands and knees.

Alison sighed. At least now that the hostage was gone, she could handle the robber as needed.

The robber forced Alison outside, her hands still on her head. She walked slowly and carefully so as to not trip, but the man hadn't seemed to realize her sight issues. More souls marked by fear, concern, anger, and even curiosity stood around the edge of the parking lot or across the street. Sirens wailed in the distance.

"It's not too late, you know," Alison told him. "You can put the gun down and end all of this before it goes too far."

The man jammed the gun against her back. She hoped he couldn't tell there was a thin magical layer between her and the weapon.

"You shut your mouth, bitch. You're my ticket out of this mess. You shouldn't have volunteered if you didn't want to be a hostage."

Alison almost rolled her eyes.

I was obviously doing it to save the woman, not because I wanted to be a hostage.

"You don't understand," Alison explained. "I'm not worried about getting hurt."

"Then what are you worried about?"

She turned her head. "*You* getting hurt."

The man scoffed. "You fucking kidding me?"

"The thing is, I really don't want to hurt you if I don't have to." Alison sighed. "But if you don't surrender, I'm going to have to. There are still too many people you might hurt."

The robber laughed and repeated, "You fucking kidding me? Do you understand the situation, you little bitch? You make one wrong move, and I fucking shoot your ass. You get me? You will die."

"Why did you even try to rob a Starbucks?" Alison frowned. "It doesn't make a lot of sense."

"I don't need to answer to you, and I'm tired of listening to your mouthy shit." The man raised his arm and tried to pistol-whip the back of her head. His gun and hand bounced off the shield, and he stumbled back. "What the fuck was that?"

Alison stood there smirking, her hands still on her head. Her shield magic was strong enough now that she'd be able to take a bullet without too much concern, but she didn't want to risk someone else getting caught in the crossfire. She'd accomplished her primary goal of making sure he didn't take a hostage who might get hurt, and it was time to end this farce of a robbery.

"Maybe the world's trying to tell you something," Alison suggested and turned around, a tight smile on her face. "You might want to listen before you end up regretting this day for a long, long time."

The robber swung his fist at her face. It bounced off her shield, and he followed up with a kick. He connected and found himself off-balance when his attack didn't send Alison to the ground. He leaned forward too far and fell to the ground as she stepped back. His gun skidded away.

Alison blasted a pulse of magic into the ground, just enough to highlight the area and the gun. She sent a thin wall of magic toward the gun. The impact shoved the weapon to the other side of the parking lot.

"You're a fucking Ori," the man growled. He stood. "I'm gonna tear you up."

Alison sighed and shook her head. "You know what Staff Sergeant Royce would say?"

"Who the fuck is Staff Sergeant Royce?"

"The man who taught me about Sun Tzu. And that's what you're missing." Alison sprang forward, not bothering to dodge as the robber threw a punch. Her shield would handle it. She threw a quick jab to his throat.

He gasped and fell to one knee.

"Here's a little move my mom taught me. It works even better with magic." Alison jumped forward, her knee out and still shielded. The man's head snapped back, and he dropped to the hard asphalt of the parking lot, groaning.

The girl shook her head and sighed. "You can't say I didn't warn you."

Loud sirens signaled the imminent arrival of the police.

Alison knelt by the semiconscious man and patted him on the shoulder. "You just got Brownstoned. I'm sure if you tell the guys you're gonna meet in jail, they'll be impressed."

She stood and hurried into the Starbucks with the help of a few magic pulses; it was harder to judge the layout without other people inside. She grabbed her suitcase and hurried toward the wall leading to the magic train.

Alison let out a sigh of relief as she passed through the wall. The dozens of souls inside and the heavy magic of the train station was a stark contrast to all the fear and anger outside. Other than a few strands of frustration and annoyance, no one in the hidden station seemed to have even noticed there had been a robbery attempt outside.

I wonder if they would have stopped it if I hadn't gotten involved, or if they even knew.

She reached into her pocket. Her Braille-adapted phone was handy enough outside the School of Necessary Magic, although some of the more recent spell and ward changes had made it fairly useless inside most of the time. She was going to have to rely on calling her dad from outside the school grounds.

Alison entered a quick text to her dad.

At the train station now. There was a minor problem but I cleared it up.

The police officer sighed as he tapped in the arrest notes into his tablet. He looked at his cruiser, where they'd secured the suspect. The man sat in the back in handcuffs, forlornly staring out the window.

Another officer smiled and nodded toward an elderly man. "Thank you for your information, sir." He headed toward his partner.

A woman stood in front of the first officer. She'd just completed a witness statement he hadn't even asked for, but the police officer didn't see a reason to not collect more information. There were still several aspects of the incident that remained unclear.

"Let me get this straight," he replied. "The guy comes out of the place with some girl with dyed white hair as a hostage—some teenager, you said—and he tries to hurt her, and not only does he not pull it off, but she beats him up? Would you say that summary is accurate?"

The woman nodded and pointed to the Starbucks. "She ran in there."

"We already checked." The police officer glanced that way. They'd even checked the bathrooms. "We found two employees in the back, including one who did mention a girl volunteering to be a hostage, but we couldn't find the girl."

"I can show you the final moments on my phone if you want." The woman held up her cell, excitement on her face.

The officer's partner shook his head. "That's not necessary, ma'am. Thank you for your assistance."

The woman offered him a polite nod and headed back toward the sidewalk where the others were standing.

They were going to review the surveillance camera footage in a few minutes. He didn't want to watch ten random shaky-cam phone videos.

The first officer turned toward his partner and frowned. "What the hell is going on? Where's the girl?"

His partner laughed. "I watched the old man's video. Just leave it alone. I recognized her immediately. You would have, too. She was all over the tv last summer."

"Who's the mystery girl?"

"Alison Brownstone."

"That explains it." The police officer chuckled and pointed to the suspect. "He's lucky he's still alive."

CHAPTER THIRTEEN

Maybe this shit is me being a dumbass? Trey thought to himself.

He frowned as he stepped out of his truck. After closing the door, he pulled out his phone to check his bounty app. The afternoon target was supposed to be a quick in-and-out pickup, so he hadn't bothered to have any of the other rotation guys come with him.

Now that he had his gloves, he'd been doing solo jobs more often. It wasn't that he thought he was James, even if he had a magic item and a truck like his mentor, but Trey accepted that he was operating at a different level than anyone else in the agency except James and Victoria.

The target, Gino Cantu, was a level two who was wanted for contraband smuggling. The man had connections with some of the local Mafia Families, but from what Trey had heard, he wasn't a full member. When Cantu had popped up on the app, Trey decided he could handle a straight level two by himself.

A few well-asked questions to informants around town had led the bounty hunter to the pleasant split-level.

Huh. Doesn't look like the kind of place a piece of shit on the run would live, but maybe that's part of the plan.

Trey pulled on his gloves and smiled. If Cantu was dealing illegal guns as part of his smuggling, the man might be packing some major heat. A hard entry would be the best strategy.

Surprise took care of a lot of the violent low-level bounties right away. When they realized they didn't have the upper hand, they often surrendered. Trey wasn't sure if he should go for shock or a more diplomatic approach.

Nah. Let's do this all direct and shit. Time to deal with Mr. Trey Garfield, motherfucker.

Trey blinked when he looked up at the house. "What the hell?"

What he saw changed everything. A young boy waved at him from a second-story window. Trey waved back, his face twisting into a frown.

I can't go kicking in a door if there is a kid in there. Fucking Cantu! Why are you on the run with a kid, you son of a bitch? That shit is dangerous.

Trey shook his head. *I ain't down with risking no kid's life. It ain't his fault his dad is a piece of shit.*

An adult-sized shadow appeared in the window and the child moved back. Someone closed the blinds.

Fuck. And Cantu already knows I'm here. Maybe he won't be a dumbass about this shit. I'm praying he won't.

Trey scrubbed a hand over his face. There was nothing worse than a bounty takedown with an innocent bystander. Most of the time, he got lucky. It turned out that pieces of trash hung out with other pieces of trash. Taking down a bounty's girlfriend who was trying to gut him with a knife while she screamed about how she was going to kill his family didn't bother him.

But every once in a while, the nightmare scenario presented itself.

Should I call the cops? If I do that, he'll just run, and the kid will still be in danger. Damn. Let's be reasonable, then.

Trey took a deep breath and headed toward the porch. He was now regretting not bringing backup. If he'd had others with him, they might be able to handle this situation quickly enough to protect the child. This wasn't a surprise wizard ambush, but it was almost as bad.

He closed on the front door and knocked. "Please answer, you dumb motherfucker."

A few seconds later, the door swung open. A dark-haired man stood on the other side—Gino Cantu.

"Who are you?" the bounty asked, looking Trey up and down, his mouth curled in distrust.

Trey gestured toward the door. "Why don't you just step out on the porch so we can talk? Don't want the kid to overhear anything he ain't ready for."

Or seeing something he ain't ready for, depending on what you say, Cantu.

Gino nodded slowly, something approaching appreciation in his eyes as he stepped onto the porch and closed the door behind him. "You're not with the Family. Obviously."

Trey grinned. "I've got my own family. So, here's the deal. My name is Trey Garfield, and I'm a bounty hunter with the Brownstone Agency. I'm here to apprehend you as a level two bounty. I don't want trouble or a kid getting hurt, so if you're willing to come along quietly, we don't have to have trouble." He nodded at the door. "He in there alone, or do we need to bring him with us?"

Gino sighed and looked down. "He's in there with his… nanny. He doesn't know what kind of man I am, so if we can do this quietlike, I'll appreciate it."

"The nanny know the deal?"

"Yeah, but she's a good woman. She only cares about the kid." His eyes widened. "Look out!"

Trey turned around in time to see the grenade hurtling toward a front window at the side of the porch. The grenade exploded, launching shrapnel and glass everywhere. By reflex, Trey threw himself over the other man. Glass shards shredded his clothes, but the defensive magic of his gloves left him with only a few cuts and bruises rather than ready for the hospital or immediately needing a healing potion.

Trey hopped to his feet and shook his head. "What the fuck?"

Gino pointed to the street.

A man in a trench coat grinned at them both. "Did I get your attention, Cantu?"

"You could have killed us," Trey shouted. "You crazy-ass motherfucker. Who the fuck are you?"

The man ignored Trey and focused on the bounty. "Gino Cantu. You're wanted for smuggling. There's level two bounty for your apprehension. You're going to come along with me." He pulled back his coat to reveal more grenades. "Or you're going to end up in pieces. I think the choice is easy."

What the fuck? Another bounty hunter?

"Are you fucking crazy, you dumb motherfucker?" Trey shouted, brushing glass shards off him. "There's a kid inside, and this ain't no dead-or-alive bounty. Besides, bitch, I was here first. You don't go jumping on a brother's bounty."

"I don't care," the other bounty hunter declared. He rested his hand on another grenade. "Cantu's a dangerous man, and I'm jamming the local cameras. When the cops show up, I'll just tell them he got frisky and I had no choice but to get extra rough. Not my fault some crazy criminal went wild and there was collateral damage. Besides, I can still get fifty percent off this one for a dead bounty."

Trey gritted his teeth. The Vegas police had warned him about this sort of thing, but he hadn't run into it before. LA had a more robust history and a better relationship between bounty hunters and police, meaning most of the local bounty hunters understood they needed to keep their operations clean. That wasn't the case in every city, which was one of the reasons the Vegas police were so interested in getting Brownstone and his people heavily involved in the city's bounties.

Trey stepped off the porch, his eyes narrowed. "Go check on your boy, Gino. I'll deal with this motherfucker."

The bounty nodded and rushed inside.

"You don't step on another man's bounty," Trey yelled. "It'd be one thing if you'd beat me here, but I was already on site. You could have killed me, motherfucker, and I don't like how you're doing things."

"Sorry, pal." The man shrugged. "Shit happens. If you've been in this game for more than a few months, you should know that." He narrowed his eyes. "You seem familiar. Have I seen you before?"

"You don't want to go to war with the Brownstone Agency."

The trench-coated bounty hunter snorted. "Oh, is that who you are? I fucking hate you guys. Ever since you've come into town, it's been harder for me to grab people. You're always there a day ahead of me or at least a few hours."

"I'm Trey Garfield. I run things here for the agency." He slammed his gloved fist into his palm. "Now walk your ass up the street before I kick it up the street, bitch."

"You going to kill me, Brownstone Boy?" The other man snorted. "Killing another bounty hunter isn't like killing the bounty accidentally. They spend a lot of time watching you. It's really fucking annoying, and it makes it hard to work. Trust me, I know. Also, never go to Orlando. Totally fucking lame-ass cops who don't understand what it means to be a bounty hunter."

Who the fuck is this asshole?

"You just threw a grenade at a house, and you didn't even know what was up before doing that." Trey glared at the man. "You're not a bounty hunter. You're just some asshole who likes killing people."

"Hey, nothing wrong with enjoying the fringe benefits of your job. You think I'm afraid of you because you run around with Brownstone?" The man reached into his pocket and pulled out a golden ring. "I heard all about how you got your ass beat down by the Silver Ghost, Garfield." He slipped on the ring, and a golden glow surrounded him. "I didn't want to waste this on some punk like Cantu, but it'll be more than enough to kick your ass back to LA where you belong. Name's Jared, by the way. You heard of me?"

Trey snorted. "No. I don't spend a lot of time asking people about weak-ass psycho pieces of shit. It upsets my stomach."

Jared advanced slowly, his fists up. "You know why I used the ring? Because I heard you've got some magic of your own, and I noticed you didn't pull a gun. That means you've got a reason to think you can beat me, even with all my grenades."

"So, let me lay this shit out of for you, motherfucker." Trey raised his fists. "I'm gonna knock your punk-ass out, then I'm gonna call the cops and have them come and pick up both you and Gino Cantu. I'm gonna explain to the cops how you tossed a grenade and could have killed my ass, and I'm pretty sure the Vegas police aren't gonna be happy with your grenade-tossing motherfucking self."

"Stop your bitching, Garfield." Jared slipped his coat off and let it fall to the ground, revealing a knife and holster underneath. "It's not like you've never killed anybody. Stop acting like a scared virgin on prom night."

"Even the big man don't just blow open a building without having a fucking clue who's inside." Trey closed on Jared, and the two men began circling each other. "And he'd give a shit if a kid was around."

"Then Brownstone's wasting all that strength." Jared rushed forward and threw a punch.

Trey blocked it and launched a wide hook of his own. The blow landed, and the other bounty hunter stumbled back a few feet and shook his head.

"Ouch." Jared wiped the blood off his mouth. "You hit hard. If I didn't have this ring on, you would have probably knocked my ass out. Good for you, Garfield. That's the only hit you're going to get in today."

"Keep talking, Jared."

Trey charged and sent a flurry of punches at the other man. Jared blocked most of them, grunting at a body blow. He retaliated with a quick kick.

Trey stumbled back, pain radiating from his chest. He was sore from the window explosion, but nowhere near enough to distract him. The adrenalin from his anger was more than enough to keep him focused. He didn't regret not using the healing portion, it would have been a waste.

Jared bounced on his feet, grinning and gesturing for Trey to attack. "You're going to regret ever coming to Vegas and messing with my turf. At first, I just thought you were some criminal piece-of-shit friend of Cantu, which is why I didn't care when I threw the grenade. Now that I know who you are, I want to take you down even worse."

"And you're going to be looking for a new dentist after I'm done with you." Trey continued to circle the man, his fists up. "You're worse than a criminal because at least they admit what they are."

Jared sneered. "You're a self-righteous asshole. I'm going to enjoy hurting you."

Distant sirens sounded.

"They're coming, Jared," Trey taunted. "And I'm still here to talk about how you're a crazy sonofabitch."

Jared growled and swung again. Trey didn't block this time. Instead, he grabbed the man's arm and slammed his forehead into the other man's nose. The other bounty hunter hissed in pain, and Trey brought up his knee.

Enjoy this, *motherfucker.*

When Trey's opponent doubled over in pain, the Brownstone bounty hunter smashed a fist into the side of his head. Trey continued to rain blows on him until Jared lay on the ground groaning, his face battered and the golden glow gone.

Jared's ring flashed and then crumbled into dust.

Trey shook out his hands. "Fuck, never thought there would be a day I'd defend some mob-connected smuggler from another bounty hunter."

The front door opened and Gino emerged, the boy holding his hand and a scared young woman standing behind him.

Trey took a deep breath. "The cops will be here soon, so we'll just wait for them. You can go with them, along with my boy Jared here."

Gino blinked as he looked at Trey and the other bounty hunter. "Thank you. I know you didn't have to be cool about this to begin with, let alone stop that guy."

"The Brownstone Agency is about taking down bounties, so you were going down. Let's make that clear. But the Brownstone Agency is also about protecting people, and we ain't good with hurting innocent kids." Trey glared at Jared. "A bounty hunter who don't care about who he hurts ain't any better than the people he's chasing for a living." He lifted his head and squared his shoulders. "And when James Brownstone was getting hunted by every mother…" He glanced down at the child and cleared his throat. "Every hitman in LA, he made sure the police knew, and he walked away from people. That's the example the big men sets."

Two police cars screamed down the street and skidded to a halt in front of the house.

Trey grinned. "Time to go to jail, Jared."

CHAPTER FOURTEEN

L yle sighed as he looked at the groaning and bloodied people around him. Some had stopped moving.

That got a little out of hand, but it was still pretty fun for me. It wasn't even like I had to make that many puppets for it to get crazy, either. Funny how that works.

All Lyle had wanted was to have a little fun at the busy corner store. Yes, he'd started a fight, and it'd spiraled out of control. The next thing he knew, he was in the middle of a riot.

He sighed and shook his head. The real lesson was something far more important.

I definitely need bodyguards. A couple of the guys almost hurt me, which wouldn't have been all that fun. The puppets are supposed to entertain the audience, not hurt the audience.

Lyle sighed as he stepped out of the store, wiping the blood off his hands. A police officer approached him, his hand on his gun.

"Oh, I took too long," Lyle muttered. "Of course you're here." He held up a hand. "You can't blame me, you know.

In truth, it wouldn't have gotten out of hand if the potential wasn't already there. I'm not going to say I'm a victim, but neither is anyone in there. Does that make sense?"

The cop frowned. "Sir, I'm going to need you to put your hands on your head for now and turn around until I stabilize and confirm the situation."

"No." Lyle shook his head. "Why should I? Because some people got hurt? You know what?" He shrugged. "Who cares? So a few people got hurt. You should just think of them as sacrifices. It's better to have sacrifices early on when the new god values them more, not when everyone's worshipping him. It's like when there's that new band you discovered before they went all mainstream and everyone claims to have always loved them. Be a true fan, man." He snickered.

The cop frowned. "Okay, sir, I'm going to need you to get on the ground right now. You're obviously under the influence or in shock, so I need you to work with me so you don't get hurt. Do you understand me?"

"Work with you?" Lyle snorted. "You don't get it, do you? Whatever." He frowned. If he tried to touch his bone charm, he might get shot. He turned around and knelt, slowly moving his hand toward the charm.

I'm tired of this. I have all this power, and I'm still treated disrespectfully. That shit ends today.

Lyle pressed on his charm. "Turn around and fire randomly at the cars in the parking lot."

The police officer spun and started unloading his gun. Car windows shattered and alarms wailed as he blasted away.

Lyle stood and laughed. "Keep firing."

The police officer ran out of bullets. "I need more ammo."

"Don't reload," Lyle commanded. "Stand there while I stun you." He walked over to the officer and yanked the stun rod off his belt, then slammed it into the man's neck and discharged it.

The other man collapsed with a groan, twitching.

"I'm tired of hiding," Lyle shouted. "I shouldn't have to fear anyone." He sneered. "No one. Don't you people understand who I am? Don't you understand how I was chosen? I was nothing, and now I'm everything."

He stuck his hands in his pocket and started whistling *If I Only Had a Brain* as he walked away.

Lieutenant Weber frowned as he read the incident report on his computer. "Do you realize what this means?" He looked over his shoulder.

McMahon stood behind him, his arms crossed. "This shouldn't be so bad. If what the cop reported was true, the guy has some sort of mind-control magic. He's probably not bulletproof, though, so we can use a few of the anti-magic deflectors to take his ass down. Remember that time Hall told us how she took down that witch who used fear magic? She said the deflector worked really well in that situation."

Lieutenant Weber shook his head. "I was looking over some of the stuff sent by the FBI and PDA earlier." He clicked his mouse and brought up an image from a traffic drone. He pointed at a Porsche sitting in front of Sarkazian's house. "They've identified that car as leaving Sarkazian's place minutes before the explosion. They've got several shots of the driver in different places, algorithmic face match at ninety-five percent. He switched vehicles a few times. He also had a briefcase when he entered Sarkazian's house, but he didn't have it when he left, so that was probably the crystals."

"Who is he?" McMahon leaned forward to peer at the image on the screen.

"Lyle Lassom. Low-level scum bag, mostly freelance, from the Providence area." Lieutenant Weber pointed at the image. "He was just a normal guy, or at least he was until a few weeks ago. Turns out he was photographed near two wizards who were being investigated by the PDA for selling dangerous Oriceran artifacts. They were found dead a few weeks ago. It looked like they'd killed each other in some sort of deal gone bad, but the follow-up investigation found evidence that they'd been preparing to sell this bone mind-control charm."

McMahon snorted. "So Lassom grabs it and decides he wants to be the kingpin, not the stooge?"

"That's what I'm thinking. The FBI is now looking into a pattern of unusual occurrences across the country starting from several weeks ago. Lassom's good at using his power, but he's not always great about covering his tracks when he's on the move."

McMahon shrugged. "The play's the same. Suit up, find him, and depend on the deflectors. If this power is from some artifact, all we need to do is get it off him, right?"

"That sounds simple, but I'm not so sure." Lieutenant

Weber brought up another video. "This is security camera footage from the store brawl." He clicked Play.

Lyle stood in the center of a chaotic mass of fighters with a huge smirk. People lay on the ground all around, as others punched, kicked, or kneed one another. He stepped forward with a glassy-eyed old woman walking right in front of him. He laughed and put his hand on his chest before saying something. The old woman walked over to a bleeding man on the ground and stomped on his neck.

A few seconds later, she pulled out a contact Taser and jammed it into his ribs. The man thrashed on the ground as Lyle threw his head back and cackled.

McMahon's face twisted in disgust. "Lassom's the poster boy for 'power corrupts.'"

"Yes." Lieutenant Weber paused the video. "If you read the PDA report on this charm, it's ridiculously powerful. It's not any subtle hypnosis stuff. You can make a person do whatever you want. Just like Lassom made that old lady stomp and Taser that guy or that fifteen-year-veteran of the force open fire at random. We were lucky he didn't hit anyone." He nodded toward his screen. "The PDA thinks those dead wizards were controlled by Lassom, too. Apparently the bone charm leaves a particular magical signature when it's used on a victim, and they found residual amounts of that where they found the wizards."

McMahon frowned. "So, we have a guy who can make anyone do anything, and he doesn't give two shits about innocent people. If we go after him, he'll probably use human shields."

"Exactly. Between the FBI, PDA, and local evidence, I'm

going to try to get an emergency level-five bounty posted. I'm nervous about that, though."

"Why?"

Lieutenant Weber sighed. "I just called Maria, and she told me Brownstone's out of town for a few days."

"He's not the only high-end bounty hunter," McMahon replied. "And we shouldn't depend on him anyway. Do we know where Lassom is right now? If we play it smart, we can surprise him and win."

"We've got no eyes on him. He switched cars again, and after the thing at the store, he was obviously trying a lot harder to avoid cameras." The lieutenant stared at Lassom's frozen image. "But you're right. We can't wait around for Brownstone or any other bounty hunter to do our job. We need to take this asshole down and fast. It might take a couple of days to get the bounty going, but if we can catch him in the meantime, fine."

CHAPTER FIFTEEN

James pulled the truck up to the small guardhouse. The tiny dull-green building lay about ten yards from the twenty-foot-tall metal fence blocking further progress. The dirt road they'd been following disappeared past the fence, grass and bushes on the side. A gate was part of the fence, and it had various complicated runes and other symbols painted all over it.

"Do they have a fence around the entire forest?" James asked. "That looks like a lot of effort to seal off one place."

Shay nodded. "Yeah. It's not just a fence, and those runes on it aren't just for show. It's got a bunch of special wards and other magic on it. They had a lot more trouble than I realized right after the gates opened, but the magic we have now helps keep the shit contained. Fortunately for them, this forest is relatively small."

"Can't shit just fly out?"

Shay shook her head. "Not the way they've got the spells set up. They extend into the air, even though the walls don't." She shrugged. "It's kind of funny. This is actually one of the more sophisticated magically sealed areas on Earth, but not a lot of people have heard about it, even though this used to be a major tourist attraction before the gates opened."

"Everyone's got magical shit around them these days." James frowned and looked at the guard house.

Are those assholes gonna come over here or not?

Two bored-looking Romanian soldiers stood inside the guardhouse, watching their phones. One of them finally looked up, and he slung his rifle over his shoulder and stepped outside to head to the truck. He sighed the entire way over as if having to move was a great imposition on him.

"Just show him the QR code," Shay told James as she handed her phone to him. "The Professor said all this shit should already be set up. I'm really hoping we don't have to try to talk our way in if this doesn't work."

James rolled down the window and held out the phone.

The soldier stopped and stared down at the phone with a frown. He pulled out his own phone and ran it over the code. His phone chimed, and a message popped up.

The soldier looked up after reading the message. "It says you are Americans?" he asked, his English heavily accented but understandable. "You speak English, right?"

"Yeah," James rumbled. "What about it?"

"I wanted to make sure you understand what I'm about to say." The soldier narrowed his eyes. "Let me make this clear, American. Our orders say we are to let you through, but we will not go in there after you, no matter what happens, until you're ready to leave. And once you leave, we're not letting you back in."

"Understood."

The soldier shook his head. "Do you *really* understand? Most who go in there die or are injured. We're here to keep watch on this entrance, but if people are stupid enough to go inside, they get what they deserve."

"We love you, too," Shay called from the passenger's seat. "Stirring speech."

The soldier snorted and nodded toward the gate. "We don't allow vehicles in. There's too much of a risk that the creatures might somehow use it to escape. You can move up to the gate and unload whatever gear or weapons you've brought with you, but it's not too late for you to turn around. You're just going to waste your life in there. Why don't you go back home, Cowboy? Go enjoy your beer and baseball."

Shay laughed. "You have no idea who he is, do you?"

The soldier shrugged. "The pass just says to let one American man and woman through with weapons and explosives." He frowned at James. "Why? Are you famous? Have you had a show?"

"I'm James Brownstone." He shrugged.

The soldier stared at him for a few seconds, then blinked. He pulled up his phone and tapped away, panic on his face. An article in Romanian about James appeared, or at least he assumed it was about him since his frowning face was at the top.

"No, no, no." The soldier shook his head, his face a mask of panic. "You can't burn it down. They've told us that. If you burn it down, the evil will spread. The magic can only contain it so well."

"Huh?" James blinked and looked over at Shay. "What

are you talking about? Burn what down?"

"The forest, I'm guessing." Shay laughed. "He thinks you're going to burn it down."

The soldier pointed at James. "That's what he does. He blows things up. The Scourge of Harriken."

"Not all that often. Mostly I punch and shoot things." James shrugged. "Or slice them up or blast right through them. I don't actually blow shit up all that often." He started counting the number of areas he'd blown up in the last year on his fingers. He lowered his hand when the number ticked higher than he'd have liked.

Okay, so maybe I blow shit up more often than I think.

The soldier gritted his teeth and looked back at his partner as if he was deciding if he wanted to attempt to stop the Scourge of Harriken from taking on the most accursed forest in Romania. He took a deep breath and gestured toward the gate, some of the panic ebbing from his face. "The same rules apply. Stop your vehicle in front of the gate and get your equipment." He muttered something under his breath in his native language as he headed toward the gate. James didn't need to know Romanian to understand that the man was cursing.

James pulled forward. "Do I really blow shit up that often? I mean, I do it more than some random asshole in an office, but I'm a class-six bounty hunter."

"'Often' is subjective," Shay responded. "You don't blow up most of your bounties. That's got to mean something."

"I've never burned down a forest."

"There's always a first time. Had you blown up a hospital before that fight with the shepherd?"

"It was already closed and abandoned. That shit

shouldn't count." James grunted as he stopped the truck in front of the gate. He killed the engine and hopped out to go to the back. The nervous soldier unlocked the gate and pulled it open. He yanked out his magazine and slipped in a red-painted one.

"Anti-magic bullets?" Shay asked.

The soldier gave a curt nod and focused on the forest on the other side of the open gate, his rifle at the ready. His partner emerged from the guardhouse, anti-magic bullets now loaded into his weapon, and advanced on the gate.

James glanced at the rifle as he opened the tailgate of the truck. Considering there were many guardhouses spread along the wall, even in areas without roads, the Romanian government was putting out a lot of money to ensure their soldiers at least had a chance against anything that might boil out of the forest.

James and Shay spent the next few minutes loading up. Standard guns and ammo, anti-magic and normal, a few frag grenades, and knives magic and normal. Shay took her *tachi* as well as her defensive pendant and ring. They slipped on canteens and backpacks that contained more ammo and several MREs. They had no idea how long they might be in the forest, and neither wanted to eat anything from a place tainted with such wild magic.

One of James' ugly gray coats served as an additional ammo reservoir. Shay filled her pouches with different single-use artifacts of various types, unsure what might be useful given they still weren't sure what all they would face.

Shay closed the back of the truck and headed toward the gate with James at her side. He reached up and felt for the amulet underneath his shirt. He hadn't bonded Whispy yet, not wanting to listen to the amulet until he absolutely had to.

I wonder if I'll even need him in the end. This place might be more hype than truth.

James stepped through the gate first, then Shay. He didn't feel anything. He'd expected a tingle or a buzz, given all the magic that was supposed to be in the place, but it felt the same as the other side of the gate.

Shit. Kind of disappointing.

"The witches put powerful magic on this gate," the first soldier explained. "You can't open it without the special key. We'll check the gate every couple of hours. If you're at the gate then, we'll open it. If not, you can yell, but if there are creatures near you, we won't open it. Our duty is to protect the country."

"Don't worry," James replied. "We won't need your help."

The soldier watched him for a moment, a hint of a smile on his face. "Let's see if a monster can defeat monsters."

The soldier pulled the gate closed and locked it, his partner still covering the forest with his gun.

James and Shay were now sealed in. Other than the dense undergrowth, it didn't seem all that different from any other forest.

"Go ahead and bond Whispy," Shay recommended as she took in the trees around them with a careful eye. She pulled a flat disc with a glowing green arrow on it out of a pouch.

James reached under his shirt and removed the spacer

from the back of the amulet. "What's that?"

"Secondary tracking artifact. This place is notorious for messing with people's sense of direction. This little baby is pair-bonded with one in the truck. It'll only last a few days, but as long as I have it, we should be able to find our way out of here. I figure it's better than leaving breadcrumbs."

"Probably." James let the amulet drop and hissed as Whispy sank into his chest and spread his tendrils.

Initiation, Whispy sent.

James took a few deep breaths.

High probability of adaptation, Whispy reported. *Unusual levels of compatible alternative energy sources detected.*

What the fuck does that mean?

Continuing baseline matrix modifications potentially compatible with alternative energy sources. Adaptation analysis possible if concentrated source found. Find enemy. Engage enemy. Achieve maximum adaptation and primary directive.

"What the fuck?" James muttered.

Shay looked his way. "What's wrong?"

"It's Whispy. He's saying all this shit about alternative energy sources if I find a concentrated supply. I don't know what the fuck he's getting at." James glanced around. He didn't feel or see anything unusual.

Shay's eyes widened. "No fucking way. This is perfect." She laughed. "Too damned perfect."

"I have no idea what the fuck you're talking about."

She gestured around. "This place. The magic. Maybe he can somehow adapt to use it."

James shrugged. "There's plenty of magic around all the time. You telling me he hasn't been able to adapt to that shit after more than thirty years?"

"No." Shay shook her head. "Everyone acts like all this magic spilled over Earth when the gates opened, when in truth, it's more like a drip. It'll take centuries for the gates to open fully, maybe thousands of years. Most places don't actually have that much concentrated magic."

"But I was on Oriceran, too."

"From what you described, it didn't sound like you were there all that long." Shay grinned. "But it's concentrated here in a weird way. Maybe using magic as an energy source requires a different sort of exposure. And—"

Shay whipped out her gun in one fluid motion and pointed it above her.

A small blue portal appeared several yards away in front of them. A few seconds later it winked out of existence.

"That's different," Shay muttered. "But I guess it's not all that surprising." She chuckled. "Don't you see? This is why he has a chance of figuring something out."

James grunted. "I wonder if that means I won't have to get as pissed."

If alternative energy source adaptation is achieved, primary power requirements will be reduced, Whispy explained.

Guess that means I won't.

James frowned. "The bastard's been doing long-term modifications ever since I took down the shepherd. I should have been asking him more about them." He shook his head. "Whatever. Let's find your crazy instrument. I might not even need my amulet abilities or any of the transformations."

Shay sighed and reached into another pouch. She pulled out a small chicken figurine atop a black base, which rotated and pointed into a dense patch of forest. "Looks like it works."

She uttered the activation phrases for her pendant and rings. Her skin started glowing silver, something that only happened when both were used together.

She marched forward, and James followed her, scanning the forest.

"You know what I don't see?" he asked, looking around.

"Birds or insects?" Shay replied. "Or any animals at all."

"Exactly. Just the trees and plants."

They continued walking in near-silence, only the jangling of their equipment keeping the quiet at bay. Whispy occasionally murmured about finding enemies, but even the amulet was acting like they were in an unnatural place and he was scared.

The forest grew denser and darker as the minutes passed, and the trees more gnarled. Trees with curved trunks became more common, and the bushes and grass grew sparser. There were still no signs of any animals.

"I wonder what weird shit is gonna jump us," James mused aloud. "No way they locked down this place without real shit to worry about."

"Yeah," Shay replied. "Peyton found a few incident reports, but mostly it was about recovering bodies after they'd been killed. From what he could find, the potential threats vary by season. All the government's attempts to use satellites, drones, and scrying magic to perform a census has failed."

A hissing, spiraling portal appeared high up and disappeared in less than a second in a puff of smoke. Another portal, this one translucent, appeared half out of the ground at a forty-five-degree angle and lingered for about five seconds.

Shay pointed up. "Stuff like that doesn't help." She gestured around. "The thing is, the trees look weird, but they are still alive, so it's not like this area sucks away life or something." She glanced down at the chicken figurine and shook her head. "I swear, the next time I see the Fixer, I'm gonna punch him in the nose. I refuse to believe this thing isn't some sort of joke."

James frowned as he looked between the trees. There were no normal trees left, every single one having a curved trunk that made them resemble upside-down candy canes. A mix of iridescent greens and dull browns dotted the leaves. The extremely patchy grass was more brown than green, although occasionally there were blood-red streaks.

He narrowed his eyes as something glowing seeped up from the ground and out of the darkened shadows in the forest. "Do you see that?"

"Yeah, I do." Shay frowned. "What is it?" She stowed the tracking instrument and grabbed the hilt of her sword.

James pulled his .45 as Whispy beamed excitement into his mind.

Engage new enemies. Achieve maximum adaptation.

The glow grew brighter as its source filled in the empty space between the trees. A dense fog of glowing particles wrapped around the trunks and stretched toward James and Shay.

Something hissed in the fog, and James aimed in that direction. Shay drew her sword with a frown as the fog thickened. The mist flashed.

Now what?

CHAPTER SIXTEEN

A*daptation in progress,* Whispy reported.

Huh? What are you talking about? I wasn't even attacked.

Adaptation in progress. Unexpected spatial displacement.

I'll worry about it later. I've got someone to chat with.

Bipedal reptilian creatures emerged from the fog. They were covered in thick dark-green scales and held swords in their clawed hands. The short, curved blades appeared to be made of a semi-reflective metal, and James wondered if they were magic.

The creatures hissed, their tongues licking the air and their slitted yellow eyes focused on James. A few let out quick screeches.

"What the fuck *are* you bastards?" James muttered. "I've got a few ideas, but you mind telling me?"

Whispy reiterated his litany of death and destruction, and the bounty hunter was half-inclined to agree. A group of creatures with weapons hadn't shown up to get ready for a dance.

In the truck on the way to the forest, Shay had mentioned something from Romanian legend called a Zmeu. In the old stories, the intelligent and dangerous creature sometimes took the form of a half-man, half-dragon. In others, they took on human form to trick their enemies. The monsters before him were good candidates for Zmeu, even if they lacked wings. Whatever they were, they didn't look friendly.

The thick glowing fog stopped its forward spread and instead started to encircle James as if it were alive.

James frowned but kept his attention focused on the Zmeu.

Extreme spike in background energy levels, Whispy announced. *Analyzing exposure to alternative energy source and integrating with previous modifications for additional power.*

"Back the fuck off," James bellowed, pointing his gun at the nearest Zmeu. "If you don't screw with me, I won't screw with you. I'm not here to fuck with you Zmeu or whatever the hell you are. I'm here to help my woman get some stupid-ass evil instrument, not clean up the magical zoo."

Additional monsters emerged from the fog, each armed with the same type of black metal sword.

Damn. Surprised Shay's been so quiet.

"These are Zmeu, right, Shay?" James called out. "Or are they something else? Should I fuck them up, or do you have a different idea?"

When Shay didn't reply, he looked to his side and growled. His heart kicked up. She wasn't there. He jerked his head back and forth, seeking his woman. The monsters surrounded him on all sides now, but there was no sign of Shay or any evidence she'd been anywhere near him.

"What the fuck did you bastards do with Shay?" James yelled. "You've got five fucking seconds to tell me or bring her back, or I will end you. Do I fucking make myself clear?"

The monsters' only response was a chorus of hisses and low screeches. A few brandished their swords.

"Don't spew that dinosaur shit at me," James called. "Back the fuck off, or I will *make* you back the fuck off."

The Zmeu spread evenly around him, raising their weapons. They gave no indication that they cared, or even understood his words. A few jogged toward him, readying their weapons and screeching.

"Time's up, assholes." James fired his .45 at a Zmeu's head. The bullet bounced off with a spark, but all the creatures leapt back, gripping their swords tighter and hissing even louder. He lowered his gun and tried to put three rounds in the creature's scaly chest, but the armor there didn't seem any more vulnerable to his gunfire than the head had.

Well, fuck.

Whispy grew excited

James narrowed his eyes. He'd expected them to charge once they realized his gun didn't work, but they'd moved backward after each shot, their tongues flicking in what he interpreted as a mixture of fear and agitation.

Afraid of guns, huh? Is that it? You get used to the Romanian Army shooting you with anti-magic bullets? But how long is my shit gonna hold you, since it doesn't even work?

The creatures continued to watch him warily, their

fingers flexing on the hilts of their weapons, but they didn't charge. If guns didn't work, it was time for something different.

James took his chance to yank out, prime, and toss two grenades into different groups of Zmeu. They exploded among the dragon men, knocking several of them down, but the creatures scrambled back to their feet with loud screeches and hisses but no obvious wounds. His frag grenades had accomplished nothing more than annoying them. Again, the attack was at least enough to keep them from launching their own.

No wonder the Romanians keep this shit locked down. Maybe I should throw in an anti-magic magazine? No, I'll save that. There might be something a lot worse than these things in these woods. I'm not here to clean out this forest. I'm here to help Shay get that damned cobza.

James holstered his gun and growled as he spun, again seeking any sign of Shay. There was neither blood nor any of her equipment on the ground, but the damned glowing fog was still surrounding them, even if it did seem less dense than before.

The Zmeu edged forward with careful steps, letting out the now-familiar mix of hisses and screeches and shaking their swords.

"Is that supposed to intimidate me? Fuck you."

James didn't give a shit about the dragon men. He needed to find Shay. He wasn't losing her to a bunch of fucking reptiles in the middle of some Romanian forest. He clenched his hand into a fist.

Sufficient power for advanced transformation.

James grunted, surprise eroding his concern. *There is?*

Additional background energy source interface achieved. Compatible with previous extended baseline matrix modifications.

That was one way to save his special ammo.

James dropped his backpack to the ground. *Let's do it, then.*

Silver-green tendrils shot from his amulet, covering his chest, legs, and arms with armor. The Zmeu leapt back, startled. A blade extended from his right arm, and he let out a low growl. The monsters hissed and pointed their swords at him, his sudden transformation throwing them off-guard.

Bet these bastards have never seen this *before.*

Although James was worried and irritated, he wasn't anywhere near as angry as he'd been during any of his previous transformations, and he certainly didn't feel the nearly mindless anger that had consumed him during his initial advanced transformation. Even in the odd situation he was currently in, the usefulness of better control of his abilities didn't escape him.

The previous anger-based system made perfect sense if he thought about it the right way. It'd seemed odd to him when he'd first achieved advanced transformation that he needed to be so furious. A mindless warrior couldn't execute good battlefield tactics, but the realization that the symbiont was supposed to be in control had clarified everything.

James was supposed to be nothing more than the Vax version of a Swiss Army Knife, along with a glorified battery. Anger didn't matter if the symbiont was focusing on the tactics. He'd upended that system by maintaining control, and now he was going around the system again by finding a new way to fuel his powers. He had no idea if it would work anywhere except this magically-damaged forest, but he'd take the advantage for the moment.

He pointed his blade at one of the Zmeu. "Where is she?" he demanded. "Where the fuck is Shay? Did you teleport her somewhere? Push her through a portal?"

If grenades or regular bullets didn't work, it was time to find out if his Vax weaponry did. He stomped forward. He'd yet to encounter anything he couldn't defeat with Whispy's help, and he doubted the Zmeu would be the first.

"Bring it, you reptile assholes," James roared.

The creatures charged, their swords held high, their keening screeches piercing. James thrust his blade at the nearest enemy, and it pierced the Zmeu's head with ease. Dark blue blood sprayed from the wound.

James yanked out his weapon and slammed an armored foot into another monster, sending it flying into a nearby curved tree.

One of the creatures managed to close the distance and slashed with its curved sword. The weapon cut through the armor on James' side, and he grunted at the throbbing pain.

The swords aren't just for show, and they aren't normal.

New adaptation in progress, Whispy announced, faint satisfaction suffusing the thoughts. *Moderate damage. Regeneration in progress.*

James stumbled as another Zmeu stabbed him in the back. He threw back an elbow, a satisfying crunch following as he caved in his attacker's face.

He wasn't sure why shooting the monsters didn't work but crushing them with his armor-covered elbow did, but at that moment he didn't care as long as it provided him another way to fight back against the horde surrounding him. A few more Zmeu appeared out of the fog.

James' wounds seeped blood, emboldening his enemies. Several of the monsters surged forward at the same time and hacked at him, and another blow cut into his arm. The next attack damaged his leg, but the wound was far shallower than any of the previous hits.

With a loud roar, the wounded bounty hunter flung out an armored arm and knocked an attacker away before slicing across another's body. He grunted. The horde screeched and banged clawed fists on their chests in defiance.

"You fuckers should have finished me off the first time if you wanted to win," James yelled.

Primary adaptation achieved, Whispy reported. *Continue to sample enemy for maximum adaptation.*

"Now you lose, assholes."

James repaid the Zmeu for his existing wounds by decapitating one of the monsters with a clean slice of his blade. Quick stabs into the chests of two others sent them to the ground hissing and gargling blood. Their heads crunched under his powerful stomps.

"It didn't have to go down like this," James offered through gritted teeth. "I just want Shay and the fucking cobza. You didn't have to attack me."

"You will die," hissed one of the monsters. "And we will feast on your flesh, human."

"So you fuckers *do* understand me." James bared his

teeth. "Where is the woman who was with me? Tell me, or I'll finish you all off."

"The forest has taken her. She will die, just like you. You've won nothing."

The monsters tried another group charge from all sides. They hacked at him with their swords, but their blades now bounced off his armor, leaving only the lightest of scratches, which repaired themselves in seconds.

James let them attack him for a long moment before thrusting his arms out to knock several of them to the ground and kicking a couple more away. "You can't fucking win."

A Zmeu leapt at James, his blade held high over his head. James impaled him in midair and tossed him to the side with a sneer.

The pain of James' earlier wounds continued to diminish as he methodically stabbed and sliced and diced the monsters swarming around him. For all the resistance of their scales to his bullets and grenades, his symbiont blade cut through them with ease.

He'd give the Zmeu credit. They were brave bastards. Stupid bastards, but brave.

Are these fuckers nanoforms, Whispy? Or are they actual monsters?

All sampled enemies are non-nanoforms. Biological origin confirmed.

Another batch of Zmeu emerged from the fog, but with each monster that arrived, the surrounding fog grew sparser and its light dimmer.

I can win this shit. Just need to keep thinning the herd.

James roared and charged the new arrivals, ignoring his

residual pain. He split an enemy in half before smashing one over his knee and cracking its head open.

The Zmeu tried to overwhelm him with sheer numbers. Some dropped their blades and leapt toward him, trying to bite his armored limbs. One sliced at his neck, drawing blood although not wounding him seriously, and James cut the creature's arm off before removing its head. His counterattack continued, his armor now coated with blue blood.

This is fucking pointless. Where the hell is Shay?

James growled and stabbed through two Zmeu with one attack. Their allies, convinced he was vulnerable, rushed him again, but he pulled his weapon out of the dying monsters with ease and slashed at the ones rushing him.

Hisses and screeches filled the air as enemy after enemy fell to the ground. The last of the Zmeu finally perished, a victim of James' armored fist this time rather than his blade. He looked around for more fog, enemies, or Shay.

James let out a low growl. The fog had completely dissipated. He was now surrounded only by piles of dead dragon men and a forest floor coated with blue slime.

Regeneration sealed the holes in his armor and closed the wound in his neck. The pain from his earlier, deeper wounds had all but disappeared, so he didn't bother to go for a healing potion. Of all the improvements in Whispy's functionality in the last year, the increased regeneration had proven one of the most useful and obvious.

Whispy's happiness from the new adaptations suffused James' mind.

You like that shit?

Engage new and stronger enemies for maximum adaptation.

With the enemy defeated, James concentrated on his surroundings. He needed to find some sort of clue to figure out where Shay had gone.

He narrowed his eyes. The density and positioning of the trees were different from when he had been with Shay.

"Damn it, I'm not in the same place. What the fuck? Am I the one who fell into a portal, not her? That was what you meant. I got teleported."

James marched over to one of the trees and frowned. If he could fall through a portal or be teleported, he could easily get lost. He needed to take precautions. He carved a large number one into one of the trees.

"Where the fuck are you, Shay?" he muttered. He glanced down at his backpack and decided to leave it on the forest floor for now. It wouldn't fit easily over his armored shoulders.

James concentrated for a moment and took deep breaths. He didn't even bother asking Whispy directly. Instead, he imagined sharp points on his elbows, and the armor responded. A few more piercing options might help him in the next fight. He suspected he was far from done with sampling the forest's bounty.

He looked around, deciding the largest number of Zmeu corpses formed an implied arrow to the source. He set off in that direction.

"Shay!" James bellowed. "I'm coming for you."

CHAPTER SEVENTEEN

"Okay, this is just fucking annoying as shit," Shay muttered. "James?" she shouted. "You out here? Where the hell are you? You better not be hiding with that armor of yours."

This is why I prefer jobs that are in old ruins. A nice contained area, not hundreds of acres of fucking trees. It's not even that big an area in terms of perimeter, but it's still annoying as fuck.

She sucked in a deep breath and slowly let it out, clenching and unclenching her hands several times. When she'd taken the job, her only concern had been the relative strength of the creatures in the forest, not being separated by random magical events.

Shay looked around and saw nothing but more damned trees. Although she had a good idea where she was, she was annoyed with the fact that she had not the faintest clue where James might be.

I thought I was so clever with the secondary tracker, but I never thought to put one on him, or vice-versa. Great, so now he could be anywhere in this forest, and that's assuming he's still in the forest.

She'd been standing with him when the glowing fog had appeared and something hissed inside it. A jagged portal appeared to their side, and the fog and James had disappeared in a flash. She had spent the last hour searching the area where the fog had appeared, but she couldn't find any trace of the bounty hunter. At one point, she'd thought she'd heard someone yell in the distance, but she couldn't place its direction and wasn't sure it wasn't the wind playing tricks on her ears.

With our luck, he's in the World in Between, but for now, I'll proceed on the assumption that he's somewhere else in this weird-ass and annoying place. No wonder the Fixer didn't want to come here. Correk, you lazy sonofabitch, I'm going to tell you that the next time we talk face to face. Isn't this shit like the very definition of your job?

"James!" Shay shouted. "Can you hear me? Get your ass over here. We've got a job to do. This isn't a fucking camping trip, and I don't have time to spend all day looking for your barbeque-obsessed ass."

Huh. I definitely don't want my wedding in or near a fucking forest. Crossing that shit right off the list.

Shay frowned and tapped her foot. Even though her fiancée instincts filled her with worry, James had already bonded Whispy, which drastically lowered the chance of him facing any real physical danger. If anything, he was probably the single most dangerous being in the forest. Between her weapons and her shields, she wasn't concerned about much either.

Should I just keep looking for the cobza and try to find James after that, or should I look for him first? I don't have a decent plan to find James other than wander around blindly.

Damn it, I'd kill for a working drone and active support right about now. Got to figure out some sort of solution that works when we are in interference situations.

Shay grimaced and dropped her hand to the hilt of her sword, her shoulders tightening. She sensed someone or something watching her from behind. Even if she'd gotten a little softer in recent months, her killer instincts never truly went away.

Whoever or whatever is watching me, it's not James.

She spun around, ready to draw her weapon, but blinked at the source of surveillance. A pale, handsome man with a dark beard and mustache stood several yards away, his hands folded behind his back and a cheerful smile on his face.

"Huh?" Shay managed.

The man's red loop-button coat, wide-legged black pants, and high boots were a few hundred years out of date, but the large sapphire set in the middle of his forehead was the most striking detail. It matched local lore concerning at least one type of creature.

Okay, I'll let him run his lines to give him a sense of security, then I'll make it clear who is in charge.

"Who the hell are you?" Shay asked.

The man opened his mouth and started talking and gesturing. Shay didn't understand what he was saying, but it sounded like the man was speaking some sort of Romanian dialect.

She grabbed her phone out of her pocket and pressed the button to turn it on, but nothing happened.

"It was worth a shot. So much for translation." Shay stuck the phone back in her pocket. Even if she'd managed to get the phone on, the chance of her getting a decent connection in the forest was likely slim to none.

Those guards had a decent connection, though. Who knows? Maybe Peyton has some ideas about boosting signals reliably.

The man eyed her quizzically and spoke a few more sentences. He gestured to her and then to him.

Even if this guy can't speak English, I bet he can lead me to the cobza or James, even if he is what I suspect.

Shay shrugged. "I speak a few languages, but Romanian, and probably an older dialect of Romanian at that, is not one of them. Sorry, pal. We're gonna have to figure something else out for communication." She pointed to her mouth and then her ear.

The man tilted his head with a frown and the sapphire flashed.

"Can you understand me now?" the man replied in perfect English, a faint hint of a New York accent, of all things, in it. "It'd break my heart if such a beautiful silver-glowing woman couldn't understand me."

Okay, that's weird, unless he's drawing off me somehow with some sort of direct translation spell. I might suppress my accent most of the time, but it's still there when I'm not being guarded.

Good thing he doesn't get what the silver glow is. I can use that to my advantage. Well, and I have this long-ass sword.

"Yeah, I can understand you." Shay frowned and kept her hand on her sword's hilt. "Who are you?"

"Don't worry about my name, beautiful if unusual maiden. You'll learn in time. First I want you to appreciate everything I have to offer."

Shay blinked. "Huh? Are you serious right now?"

The man smiled but remained stiff, his hands still behind his back. "It's rare that I see a striking and unusual beauty such as you enter this place. I don't know why you would disguise your natural gifts with such mannish clothes, but they don't conceal the glories of your feminine form and face. I see you've received magical blessings from others, but I can provide more; much, much more."

Shay rolled her eyes. This was so not helpful, especially if the man was what she suspected.

"Look, your lordship or whatever, I don't have time for this," Shay replied. "I'm already spoken for, and I need to know where James is. You might have seen him already. He's got on a bulky gray coat. Big guy. Lots of tattoos. He might be wearing something that kind of looks like silver-green armor."

"James?" the man echoed. "This crass James can't provide you what I can, even if he is a warrior. I can give you a life of wonder and riches and introduce you to nobles, and even the king." The last few words came out uncertain. "Or whoever the grand leaders of your homeland are." He nodded, the full smile returning to his face.

Ok, you've only got the one spiel, and you're still learning to adapt it for modern times, aren't you? I wonder if that means you've been waiting around a long time or just don't see people all that often.

I suppose it doesn't matter, but if this wasn't an artifact raid, I'd love to ask you more questions.

"I…" Shay frowned and stared at the man, her eyes narrowing. No reason to let someone continue with obviously suspicious behavior. "Why won't you show me your hands? You've had them behind you the entire time."

The man scoffed. "It's more elegant than simply letting them hang to the side like a commoner. I'm showing you respect."

Shay shook her head. "Show me your hands. That's how you'll show me respect."

The man's face twitched and he lowered his hands to his sides. Long white gloves covered his arms almost up to his shoulders, but the fingers in the gloves were unnaturally long, and she assumed the fingers inside were too. Unusually long fingers in human form were another legendary characteristic of the type of creature she suspected he was.

Damn. The Romanians apparently got a lot of shit right. Wonder why the vampire shit seems so off? Maybe the vampires were aliens, and they left back in the day.

"Is this sufficient?" the man asked, with a deep frown and offense in his eyes. "A suspicious manner doesn't suit a beautiful woman."

"Wait, are you seriously trying to tell me you think a woman shouldn't be suspicious of a random weird guy in the middle of a forest with a reputation like this one has?" Shay laughed. "Oh, come on. Even *you* can't believe that makes any fucking sense, given the circumstances."

The man sneered. "You have a very active tongue, woman. A very foul one, at that."

Shay shook her head. "See, here's the problem, asshole. You're used to dealing with a different sort of woman. I'm sure your spiel worked on peasant girls in the twelfth century or whatever, but I'm a modern woman, and I'm already engaged. I'm actually surprised you haven't updated your tactics a lot better, but you could have just woken up, for all I know." She waved a hand. "Not only that, but I know what you are, so if you don't want to get your ass kicked, Zmeu boy, you better back the fuck off and help me out. I'm not here to cause trouble, but that doesn't mean I can't bring it." She patted her sword hilt.

The man scoffed. "Spare me. You aren't able to use that blade. Beautiful women spend their time and effort concentrating on frivolities such as makeup and fashion. You're no warrior."

"Believe what you want, but yeah, I'm no *warrior*. I'm a tomb raider, and I used to be a killer."

The man's face twisted into a hungry grin. "And you claim to know what I am?" He looked her up and down, a mixture of fascination and faint irritation on his face. "What kind of creature are you, then? Your silver glow comes from some sort of beauty spell, I assume, and I doubt you're a human if you know what I am and show such little fear. Are you trapped here as well?"

Shay shook her head. "I'm not trapped here. I came from the outside. I'm looking for something—a magical cobza. Would you happen to know where it is? Maybe we could cut some sort of deal." She held up a hand. "And, no, before you ask, I can't get you out of here. If I tried, soldiers with anti-magic weapons would kill you."

"You want to make a deal?" The man laughed. "You don't understand what your position is, do you, girl? I don't care what frivolous power you think you hold." He licked his lips. "It's been so long since I've tasted succulent flesh. Maybe longer than I thought if I understand what you're saying. I'm sorry, but you must die. If you come here right now, I'll take off your head so you won't suffer. That's my mercy, and that is the only deal I'm offering you."

"Will you now?" Shay raised an eyebrow. "How generous of you."

"Yes. I don't know what has happened, but I'm hungry. So hungry." The jewel flashed, and the outfit disappeared. A dark-green bipedal reptile replaced the man. He held up one hand and a black metal sword appeared in a puff of thick, dark smoke, a faint pungent odor accompanying the smoke.

"So you *were* a Zmeu in the end." Shay sighed. "I was hoping for something cooler, but I also assumed your kind would infest these woods, from my research."

"You came here knowing there were Zmeu? I don't know if I should praise your bravery or mock your stupidity, girl."

"I wouldn't worry about it." Shay smiled. "It's not gonna matter very soon."

"That is true, girl." The monster flicked its tongue. "Now come. If you don't, I'll eat you while you're still alive. I find it spoils the meat when the victims scream too much, but I'm also very hungry, so make this easy on both of us."

Man, this asshole is really asking for it. It's like someone recreated Durand in reptile form.

Shay sighed and walked toward him. A few jagged cracks appeared in the air several yards away, but they vanished without moving either person.

"Yes," the Zmeu hissed. "Give in to your fate. You can't fight me. You must know that, foolish girl. Did you seek a glorious death at the hands of my kind? Is that why you truly came here?"

"I told you that I came here to get a cursed cobza, but now I'm going to make the forest a little safer for the next person." Shay burst into a sprint, drawing her sword as she ran. The Zmeu brought his own weapon up, but it was too late. She swung her blade at his neck, and his head flew off and landed in a nearby bush. His body fell forward and hit the ground with a soft thud.

"That's what you get for thinking the sword was for show, and I took your head so you didn't suffer," she muttered. She frowned. "Wait. You didn't think it was for show, did you? You just thought you'd be immune to it. No wonder you weren't afraid." A cold snicker followed. "But none of that solves my earlier problem. There's no way something like you took James out, so that means he's here somewhere." She sheathed her sword and considered her options. "But where?"

I've got no good way to track James directly, but I can both get to the cobza and back to the main gate.

Screw it. James is a big boy. I'll concentrate on recovering the instrument, then run to any screams of the dying when I hear them because that's where he'll be. Or he'll catch up.

Shay nodded, satisfied with the new plan.

CHAPTER EIGHTEEN

Trey let out a contented sigh as he shifted under his blanket, Zoe's warm, soft body next to him in the bed. No matter what happened in Vegas, he was happy that he was able to wake up every morning next to the witch. It'd be a good day. He could feel it.

There won't be any crazy-ass bounty hunters or other assholes messing with me today. I just know it. Great day to be alive and working a job I love.

Zoe's hot breath fanned his ear.

Now what's she up to?

"Trey, wake up," Zoe whispered. "I need you."

He yawned and picked up his phone. Seven am. Earlier than he wanted to get up that day, but not crazy. They hadn't stayed up late the night before.

"Damn, baby," Trey replied. "I know you want some of this, but I think I need a little breakfast first before anything goes down. Fair enough? I need my protein to fuel my stamina."

Zoe laughed quietly. "I always want some of you, my

little supernova, but in this case, I've woken you up because someone has tripped the external wards and is coming toward the front door. I'm not expecting anyone. Are you?"

"No." Trey sat up with a frown, his heart rate kicking up.

"Whoever they are, they lack magic," Zoe replied, still smiling. "So I'm doubtful they are of any serious concern, but you should still be careful."

"Yeah, I'll be careful. If this is real trouble, I'm gonna be seriously pissed off. They should know better than to fuck with a man at his home, and this was supposed to be my nice day to wake up."

Trey grabbed his gloves from the nightstand and slipped them on, his current look ridiculous since he was only wearing boxers. He rolled out of bed and grabbed a gun from Zoe's closet. That and the gloves would be enough to defeat most common thugs; Zoe had already confirmed that the enemy wasn't magical.

Hope they didn't let that motherfucker Jared out. He'd best not be coming for vengeance, or we're gonna need a more permanent solution.

Someone knocked with loud urgency at the front door.

Trey's frown deepened. "Damn it."

He headed toward the living room as the new arrival knocked again, this time even louder.

"Hold on, I'm almost there," Trey shouted. He stepped to the side so he wasn't lined up with the front door. He wanted to make sure no one would open fire now that they'd confirmed someone was inside and close by.

No bullet storm came. That was promising. A soft knock came instead.

Don't let it be Jared or any of my informants. Or, fuck, even one of the boys.

That last didn't make sense once he thought of it. Any of the other bounty hunters in the agency would just call him.

Unless some really big shit was going down.

Trey arrived at the door and looked through the peephole. Three large men in suits stood outside, the one in the center wearing a tie and the guys on either side sporting gold chains. Trey recognized one of the chain men as local Mafia, so he assumed the other two were the same, or at least closely allied.

He sighed and shook his head. It wasn't as bad as he'd feared, but it was nowhere near "no big," like he'd hoped.

What the fuck? Did I sell the Mafia out in a previous life or some shit? Is that why they're so far up my ass lately?

He considered that thought. While Vegas did have an unusually large concentration of Mafia, particularly Italian Mafia, the post-Oriceran chaos had led to opportunities for organized crime. It wasn't like LA lacked such groups, but somehow the Family men in Vegas seemed far more interested in irritating Trey.

Huh. James has been working LA for so long that maybe those assholes are just used to staying out of the way of all things Brownstone.

Trey hid his gun behind his back as he opened the door. "It's too early in the morning to sell me cookies, guys. You'll need to come back later when I'm awake and hungrier."

The man in the center, whom Trey still didn't recognize despite trying to place him, chuckled. "We apologize for the early arrival, Mr. Garfield, but we thought this approach would be best. It lowers the chance of other shit happening, such as dangerous misunderstandings, especially with people in our line of work." His gaze dipped to Trey's visible hand, and he frowned slightly. "Or with you, for that matter."

"I don't know about all that, but what's this about?" Trey asked. "If this is about starting something, I really, really wouldn't recommend it. You guys can't win at this range."

"No, nothing of the sort. Like I said, we want to avoid any misunderstandings. My boss has made that very clear." Mr. Tie raised his hands in front of his chest. "We mean no harm. Really, pal. Far from it." He cleared his throat, a nervous look on his face. "Now, I'm going to reach into my jacket and grab a card for you. I'm telling you that because you seem a little jumpy. I'm guessing those gloves on your hand are the magic ones people have been talking about, and you obviously have your gun behind your back and are itching to shoot us."

The other two men tensed, and their hands moved, but Mr. Tie threw up his hand and they stopped.

"What are you idiots doing?" the mobster asked, frowning. "We didn't come here for that."

Trey looked at all the men and nodded slowly. "What would *you* do if three random guys showed up at your house early in the morning?" He narrowed his eyes on Mr. Tie. "Especially when you already have a rep and people have challenged it, mainly Family men."

The man sighed and shrugged. "Probably the same. Can I get the card now?"

"Yeah, but slowly."

The Mafioso reached into his jacket and inched out a business card. He held it out in his palm.

Trey snatched the card with his free hand and glanced down at it, now even more confused. "This is just a hand-written address and time. What the fuck does it mean?"

"The date of the meeting is tonight," the mobster explained. "You're to come alone, or the meeting is off."

"The meeting for what? I don't know about no meeting." Trey frowned. "With who? And why?"

"It's to your advantage to come to the meeting. No obligations will be incurred for coming, so it's win-win for you." The mobster shrugged, a bored look on his face. "Coming would be the smart move anyway. I was ordered to not say anything more than that, and I always follow orders."

Nah, it's the fucking opposite. It's like I'm Mafia catnip all of a sudden. Or is this shit about taking down Cantu? They pissed that I messed with their operation? But if they were pissed, they'd probably just try to gun my ass down right here. They have to know I'm gonna be well equipped and expecting trouble at this little meeting. Or are they depending on that shit?

Trey grimaced as he tried to think through all the permutations of the scenario in his head then decided the Mafia probably wasn't playing that sophisticated of a game.

The mobster cleared his throat. "So, you coming? I need to tell my people if you are. If you're not sure, just say yes. That will make things work out better for everyone."

Trey snorted. "What happens if I don't show up? Or if I bring someone?"

"Then you'll be disappointed and throw away something useful for no good reason." The mobster shrugged. "This isn't about trying to kill you, Garfield. Everyone's already learned that lesson. This is about something else entirely."

"Fine. I'm coming," Trey offered with a shrug. "But I reserve the right to get the fuck out of there if I smell a trap, and I guarantee I'll be taking at least three or four guys with me if it *is* a trap."

The mobster nodded. "Of course." With a final nod, he turned and walked away, the other two men following.

Trey watched them until they got in their black SUV and pulled away, then closed the door. Zoe stepped into the living room in a green silk robe, her thighs flashing with each movement. Normally he'd be turned on, but he was too confused about what had just happened to care about that.

"Did you overhear that shit?" Trey asked.

Zoe nodded. "I did."

"What do you think? Because *I* don't know what to think. I don't get why the mob's doing all this need-to-know spy shit all of a sudden." Trey shook his head. "I get that they might want to hold back a few details, but that was on a whole other level."

"I think it wouldn't hurt for you to attend their meeting." Zoe smiled and sat on the couch. She crossed her legs. "There was nothing in their arrival or pitch that suggested hostility. There was not even an implied physical threat from what I can tell, and I'm very good at reading people."

"Those two guys went for guns."

"Yes, after they realized you already had yours out. *You* created the hostility in that situation."

Trey shrugged. "People know who I am, and people know I'm living with a witch. They might have just figured it was a dumbass move to try to attack or threaten me where I live because of magic and shit. That might be why there was no hostility."

"Maybe, but I don't even think there was concealed hostility, at least not from the speaker. His manner was easy. Grateful even." Zoe tapped her lips. "I don't know what they want to discuss, but I doubt it involves any threat to you. It probably is some sort of real opportunity. Whether it's legal, who knows?"

Trey set his gun on the coffee table and sat on the couch next to the witch. "Mobsters just don't show up at a brother's crib without some sort of reason to throw opportunities at them. Maybe this is more of them trying to do that alliance shit. I'm not trying to pick a fight with the mob, but they've got to understand the Brownstone Agency won't be their bitches either because they ask all nice-like."

"Then go to the meeting and make that clear." Zoe uncrossed her legs and crossed them the opposite way. "Perhaps this is just them paying their respects to you in their own way. Even if the Brownstone Agency will not formally ally with them, they might wish to at least convince you that they are a resource or something like that."

"Bounties are bounties." Trey shrugged. "There ain't gonna be a situation where the mob suddenly gets a free pass."

"There's nothing wrong with explaining that to them, either." Zoe smiled softly. "The truth is, you'll never know what they want if you don't go to their meeting. I'll give you a few more potions to ensure your safety. If they try anything, you can escape and then gather reinforcements to punish them."

Trey looked back down at the card. "This shit's gonna interfere with our date tonight."

Zoe chuckled. "I've suffered far worse disappointments in my life, my little supernova."

"Fine. I'll check and see what these Mafia bitches want." Trey frowned at the card. "But this shit better be worth it."

CHAPTER NINETEEN

*F*ind and engage new stronger enemies, Whispy demanded.

James laughed.

You know, Whispy, you're like a fucking drug addict. I find someone powerful and we fight, and you do your adaptation thing. You're happy for like five minutes, then it's back to demanding I find more people.

Achieving maximum adaptation requires maximum sampling.

James nodded. *It's fine this time. That's why I came along. You're right. Every new adaptation makes me more of a badass, and we're gonna probably need that to complete the primary directive of destroying all Vax symbionts. If they never come here, there are plenty of Council wannabes and shit like them to take down.*

Primary directives in conflict.

Then just do what I fucking say. James grinned. *Your new primary directive is, obey James Brownstone.*

Link error acknowledged.

James snorted. That was the symbiont's way of complaining about not being in control of the partnership.

His smile faded. *Are they coming? The Vax?*

Pulse not initiated.

Could they come anyway? What happens if a Forerunner gets his ass handed to him? Or he's killed? That's got to happen sometime.

Purifier will be dispatched or system will be marked forbidden.

James stopped with a frown. *Why didn't you ever tell me that shit before?*

Primary directives in conflict. Memories stored.

He let out a long, low growl and started walking again. *So they could come. I'd half-convinced myself that they wouldn't. When will they send a Purifier? How long do they wait?*

Unknown, Whispy responded.

James walked a few feet and kicked at a blackened stump. "I better let Johnston know about this shit. Too bad it's gonna ruin his fucking day when I do."

Now that the government knew that James was an alien, he saw less reason not to share information with them when it was relevant to the safety of the country. Shay was right. While he didn't trust most of the government, in the end, if the Vax came, the military would have to play a role in defending the country and the planet. The more the government knew about the possible threat, the better they could prepare.

Even if he achieved the adaptations he needed, it'd be idiotic to place the fate of all of Earth and possibly Oriceran in his hands alone. For all he knew, some sniper might blow out his brains at a barbeque competition when he wasn't bonded to Whispy.

James had even briefly thought about whether he should have agreed to go to the Nine Systems Alliance a few times in the last few months before deciding that would have been an equally stupid plan, especially since the Alliance didn't seem to have a reliable method of beating the Vax except at the earliest stages of an invasion.

It might not be a good idea to depend solely on him to defend the planet, but James might potentially be the Earth's last line of defense if the Vax did come looking. He had no reason to believe they wouldn't come to Earth or Oriceran looking for him if he never sent off his Forerunner pulse. If anything, it seemed like the opposite would occur.

How does a system get marked forbidden? James asked

Unknown, Whispy responded.

You're not just fucking with me, are you?

Unknown, Whispy insisted.

Oriceran's not safe, James thought to himself. *My parents sent me there first, so I have to worry about* both *damned planets.*

Whispy didn't say anything for the next several minutes. His mental presence seemed cold and distant, almost like when he was in his quiescent mode, but James continued walking, still in advanced mode, through the dense trees. He'd marked several of them to help him navigate and avoid getting lost.

So far, he'd found no evidence that he'd been walking in circles or had teleported, but he also had no idea what direction he should have been walking in.

Worst-case scenario is that I just keep walking one direction. I'll eventually hit the wall, and I can find a gate from there to work my way back to the first one.

James wasn't sure how much time had passed when he came upon a small clear blue pond nestled beneath a huge tree. Unlike most of the trees he'd seen in the deep forest, this one lacked any deformities. Other than having unusually bright red leaves, it seemed like a normal, albeit large, tree.

The presence of the healthy tree and water was unusual in itself compared to what he had seen during his time in the forest. In addition, most of the nearby grass was as bright a red as the leaves on the tree.

This looks like something special, but what is it? And is it going to be annoying?

Find and engage new enemies, Whispy ordered.

At least *something* was back to normal. James didn't know how many secrets the damned symbiont was still holding, but at this point, it didn't matter much. They agreed that he needed to get stronger, so the partnership would continue.

James smacked his lips. The sight of the water was making him thirsty, but he wouldn't risk drinking from the pond. If it wasn't poisoned or tainted, it was probably enchanted. He grabbed the canteen off his belt and took a sip.

The water stirred, and the top of a head with long, dark hair broke through the surface.

His pulse quickened.

"Shay?" James called. He didn't know why she had been hiding in the water, but he was happy to have stumbled onto her. "What's going on?"

He frowned a few seconds later. A beautiful naked woman slowly rose from the water, her drenched hair pasted to her body. She continued rising until she stood atop the water, with no visible means of support.

Most men would be excited by the sight of such a gorgeous being in the middle of nowhere, but the only thing she was stirring in James was annoyance. Whoever this woman was, she wasn't Shay, and she'd gotten his hopes up, even if it wasn't her fault or intention. It pissed him off, and he'd already had an annoying enough time in the forest. He wasn't feeling generous.

The woman crooked her finger and offered James a winsome smile. She ran her other hand down her side.

Engage enemy, Whispy suggested. *Adaptation potential moderate.*

Not gonna kick her ass until I'm sure she's an enemy. She's not charging me with a sword, so I'm gonna at least give her the benefit of the doubt. But there is *something she's doing that's pissing me off.*

James cut through the air with his blade. "Knock that shit off right now. Do I look like I'm in the mood?"

The woman blinked and lowered her hand, surprise on her face.

"I don't know if you're a succubus or a leanan sidhe or some weird-ass seduction bug or something, but whatever plan you have, I'm not falling for that shit." James slammed his blade into the ground. "I've got Shay, for one thing, and I've already been told how fucked up this forest is, so I'm not trusting anything or anyone I see. That clear? As long as you understand that, we don't have to have any trouble. I'm not here to start shit with every random-ass magical creature who lives in this forest. I'm just here to find something. Maybe you could help me find it?"

The woman let out a long sigh and started speaking. He didn't understand the language. It sounded very melodic, and more like Light Elf than any human language.

Whispy, can you translate that shit?

No. Ability outside modifiable range for base matrix.

James frowned in disappointment, but the limitation made sense. The amulet could perform all sorts of physical modifications, but understanding a language wasn't just about changing a few physical traits as far as he could figure out.

He shrugged, which looked all the stranger given his armor and blade, and pointed to his mouth and then his ears. "I can't understand you. I don't understand the words coming out of your mouth."

The woman said something else and pointed at her mouth.

"Yeah." James nodded. "I can't understand you. Don't speak your language." He said the last two sentences louder and slower.

He chuckled at a stray thought. Whispy's trick to get him into advanced mode without him being filled with rage was making it easy for him to maintain and even have conversations in here. Right now, he was more mildly annoyed than anything else. That would make every encounter in the forest that much safer while he still maintained full control.

Will your alternative power trick work outside this forest? James thought.

Unknown at this time, the amulet responded.

We'll have to test that shit out later.

The woman sighed and ran a hand over her mouth. "Do you understand my words now, great warrior?" She had a vaguely French accent, but whatever she had been speaking before was definitely not French.

James didn't linger on that thought. Linguistic mysteries weren't important when Shay was still missing.

"Okay, I can understand you now," James replied. "Is this where you give me the big seduction speech in English? Because it won't make any difference. I've been hit on by all sorts of magical women, so don't think I can't resist. You're just the latest in a long line of people who want a piece of me. Don't waste either of our time."

"How unfortunate." The woman pursed her lips. "But, yes, it's obvious to me that such efforts would be wasted on a man like you. That said, we could still come to another sort of arrangement, so I'd like to offer you something else."

"And what's that?" James looked around the area for potential reinforcements or ambushes.

"A deal." The woman lowered most of her body into the water until only her head remained. "I am a lele."

James frowned. "Shay mentioned those. A type of nymph creature in Romanian folklore. You're supposed to be all seductive and shit."

He wasn't honestly sure if he didn't find her seductive

that day because she was simply bad at her job, because he was bonded to Whispy, or because he was in love with Shay. When he'd spent time around Anna Forsythe, her seductive aura had had some effect on him, so it suggested he wasn't totally invulnerable to such powers.

"That summary is accurate enough." The lele crossed her arms over her chest under water and stuck out her bottom lip. "And most men find our seduction attempts quite welcome. You're an unusual man."

"Isn't the first time someone has said that to me, but who gives a shit about that? You're not attacking me, and you're offering me a deal. I'm listening. What's your offer?"

The lele tilted her head and smiled. "As you appear to be a great warrior. I'm wondering if you could handle a problem for me. It is one that will require the strength and endurance of a true champion."

James pointed with his thumb over his shoulder. "If it's about all those Zmeu, I wasted a bunch of them. Maybe all of them."

The lele laughed. "How wonderful. You're exactly what I thought. What you've done is helpful, but that's not what I was going to ask you to do. There's another creature that needs to be slain."

"I'm a bounty hunter, not an assassin." James glared at her. "I'm not going after someone unless I get paid and I have a good reason to believe they're a piece of shit, or they mess with me. The reptile assholes attacked me, so I fought back. That's why they're all dead."

The lele's hand reappeared above the surface holding a large diamond. "Will this suffice for payment? It's my understanding that humans value such things far more than simple coin, but it changes at times."

James eyed the diamond. "I'm listening, but I also want you to help me find Shay. She's the dark-haired human I came into the forest with. From what I was told, you lele can see all sorts of shit through trees and water and crap."

"That's true." The lele nodded. "And I'm willing to do that, provided you help me with my problem, warrior."

"James," he rumbled. "James Brownstone. What's your problem, then?"

He thought about asking the lele for help with the cobza, but Shay's artifact would let them find it anyway. The less he was entangled with strange Romanian forest creatures, the better.

"I'm trapped in this place," the lele murmured. "I have been for decades now. That doesn't bother me much, and most of the others I've encountered here are reasonable, even if they don't have the exposure to humans they desire. There is one particular creature that is unnecessarily vicious and cruel. I blame him for our imprisonment here since he killed the most humans of any of the creatures, and he now preys on the rest of the creatures at times."

James scoffed. "So what is the thing? A Zmeu?"

The lele frowned and shook her head. "No, a balaur."

James locked gazes with her. "Now, I just want to be clear. From what Shay told me, a balaur is basically a dragon with more than one head?"

"Yes." The lele nodded again. "This balaur has three heads."

James chuckled.

How's that for new strong enemies, Whispy?

Whispy's anticipation was almost palpable. Even James was a little excited. He'd fought a lot of monsters in his time, but he'd never taken on something like a dragon. There was nothing wrong with a man wanting to test himself.

"Okay," James replied, "and if I help kill this thing, you'll pay me with the diamond and help me find Shay? There's no other hidden tricks or riddles or shit like that?"

The lele nodded. "No. You simply need to kill the balaur. If you've successfully fought so many Zmeu, I suspect you have the power to succeed."

"And if I don't?"

"Then the balaur will take your life." The lele shrugged. "And the situation will remain unchanged for me."

James pointed his blade at her. "You're the one who can sense my warrior spirit or whatever shit, so you should know you'd better not fuck with me over this. If I do this job, I expect payment."

"I have no reason to deceive you, James Brownstone. I will benefit greatly if you slay the balaur."

CHAPTER TWENTY

Two things struck James as notable as he followed the now-silent lele through the forest. First, there was something both absurd and amazing about a man encased in alien biomechanical armor stomping through a forest after a naked nymph as part of a plan to kill a three-headed dragon. Every bounty hunt or tomb raid with Shay, he always wondered if he'd hit the limit for new experiences, and yet he often ran into something new. That didn't even include alien artifacts or the fact he'd only been to Oriceran a handful of times.

Second, he'd thought the trees in the deep forest were crooked and twisted before, but as the minutes passed and they traveled toward his pick-up bounty, the branches on the increasingly blackened and fungus-infested trees around them grew steadily more gnarled. There was only the occasional normal tree now.

Never thought this place could get more messed up than it already is. No wonder the Romanians want to keep it locked down.

Whispy alternated between periods of quiet and near silence to issuing excited orders to James about fighting the upcoming enemy.

I wonder where Shay is right now? Since she's got the pendant, ring, and tachi, *she's at least safe.*

James nodded to himself, satisfied. "It was a good engagement ring."

The lele looked over her shoulder curiously. "What?"

"My fiancée. Her engagement ring works as a shield." James shrugged.

The lele turned back around. "Do many assassins seek the life of your woman?"

"It's not so much assassins as that she ends up in a lot of dangerous situations. Kind of like wandering around a cursed forest."

The lele sniffed disdainfully. "This place is not cursed. It's blessed."

"Blessed? You're taking me to go kill some weird-ass monster. Zmeu were running around trying to eat people. You think it's blessed?"

"You wouldn't understand, warrior. You're not a magical being, even if you use magical items such as that armor."

James didn't feel the need to clarify the nature of his armor.

The lele sighed. "For so long, this world was all but devoid of magic. It was hidden in the shadows. Many of us were forced to cluster around kemanas, desperate to live off the residual magic stored there like sad, pathetic visitors who didn't belong on this planet. Then the gates re-opened and magic began its return, but it's still only a trickle; a mockery for some of us." She took a deep breath, her eyes half-closed. "But in a place like this, the magic flows strong and directly. It shows us what could be."

James grunted. "Again, all the fucking monsters make it seem like it's dangerous."

"That's only because they've trapped so many here." The lele shook her head. "If we were all free to wander everywhere, it'd be different. You wouldn't understand, human." She sniffed disdainfully.

"Why not go to Oriceran?"

"I was born in this land. I will die in this land. I am part of the water. Part of the trees. Oriceran is not my home. Earth is, and this land is, and I welcome the magic that would spill forth."

A triangular portal opened over a branch, slicing it in half. It fell to the ground, hitting the moldering fallen leaves.

The lele cleared her throat. "That isn't to say a few things couldn't be improved."

James frowned, eyeing the cleanly sliced branch as they walked past it. "Does that kind of shit happen a lot?"

"A lot?" The lele looked over her shoulder, her hair as wet as it had been when she'd first left the pool. "Portals appearing, yes, but dangerous portals like that are rare. It gets worse the closer you go to some places. I think that is why the balaur chose the location for his lair. I believe he enjoys such chaos."

James pointed to a fallen tree in the distance, and then another. "There are lots more downed trees here. Is that from the portals too?"

The lele shook her head. "That's from the balaur. He

enjoys knocking things down. He's a newer resident of this forest. He came in through a portal shortly after the gates opened."

"And what about you? How long have you lived here?"

"About two centuries."

So, this is really about some scummy new guy who moved into the neighborhood who you want removed.

James nodded slowly as they continued toward the balaur, half-wondering if the whole thing was a trap, but he was having trouble coming up with reasons the lele would go out of her way to participate in such a plan. It wasn't like the denizens of the forest kept up with current events by watching tv or surfing the net. He was just another outsider she didn't know from anyone else.

Another few minutes passed before the lele slowed, her face and body tense. A large swath of trees that had been knocked down surrounded them. She pointed ahead in the direction they'd been walking. "He's that way. There's a cave. If you'd excuse me, warrior, I intend to hide until this is over. If you survive, I shall return with your payment and lead you to your woman." She turned and hurried off in the opposite direction with surprising speed.

James shook his head. "The weird shit I get involved in! Aliens, water nymphs, and fucking reptile guys. I wouldn't believe the movie if they made it." He advanced in the indicated direction.

What about extended advanced transformation? he asked the amulet, unsure how much trouble the coming enemy would be.

Insufficient power at this time. Further base matrix modification needed.

But I'm barely pissed off and you managed an advanced transformation.

Insufficient power at this time, the amulet repeated. *Further base matrix modification needed.*

The implications for his ability to use his suit outside a highly magically charged area were questionable, but he wasn't that worried. Every time he'd needed more power it'd been available, and as Shay had pointed out, it wasn't like he'd hurt any of his allies even when he was borderline berserk.

A man never knew on a given day if he was going to need to kill a Romanian dragon monster or an alien.

A dead zone spread out from a large opening leading into a nearby hill. Flat, cracked earth spread from the front, and hollowed-out tree trunks littered the ground. It was as if the cave was sucking the life away from everything around it.

James stopped about thirty yards away from the cave. "Hey," he yelled. "You in there? I've got an ass-kicking scheduled for you unless you can give me a reason why I shouldn't."

Engage and kill the enemy, Whispy demanded.

Almost ready to, Coach.

The cave entrance shook and rocks fell from the mouth as heavy thudding footsteps echoed from within.

James walked toward the cave. "Looks like our guy is coming."

A serpentine neck covered in black scales topped by a squat jet-black reptilian head with deep red eyes with slitted pupils poked out of the cave. Two more heads joined that one a moment later. The dark scales covered the body, and six thick legs propelled the monster forward. Though two spindly wings protruded from the back, they were so thin and hole-filled that James doubted the creature could fly, but that was assuming the wings didn't generate some sort of magical field or some other less obvious means of flight. He didn't know half the time with magic.

Once out of the cave, the balaur bellowed from all three mouths which were filled with razor-sharp teeth. The creature stomped toward James. With its heads fully extended, the creature stood over twenty feet tall.

Engage and kill the enemy, Whispy demand. *Moderate adaptation potential estimated.*

Maybe. It's just a big monster in the end.

"You talk, or you just a beast?" James yelled.

All three balaur heads roared. The farthest left head reared back and opened its mouth.

James snorted. "Gonna breathe fire? Good luck. That shit isn't going to work."

A blinding ball of white light blasted from the mouth and struck James, knocking him backward. He landed hard, his clothing smoking and his muscles twitching as electricity arced over his body. He grunted and staggered up, slightly dizzy but not in much pain. A blackened scorch mark covered the armor over his chest.

Near maximum adaptation previously achieved for attack type, Whispy reported. *Adaptation potential minimal. Kill enemy. Find and engage new and stronger enemy.*

Yeah, I think that was an electrical attack. Can't say I was expecting that.

The second head reared back, and a more traditional

stream of flame blasted from its mouth toward James. He threw up an arm to protect his head. Even if he was still partially protected due to his symbiont, without his helmet, it was a vulnerable spot.

James growled as a few remaining blackened fragments of his shirt drifted away on the now-hot air. There were mild burns in the few places his skin was exposed, including his head, but the armor was only scorched.

"Now you're just pissing me off." James hissed as stinging air touched his burns. With Whispy's ability to regenerate him, he knew the wounds wouldn't be a problem soon. It was time to show his enemy why no one tried to fry James Brownstone.

The monster issued an almost barking noise from its third mouth.

James ran toward the balaur's side. "They should just call you a three-headed dragon or a hydra or some shit. Everybody's got to have their own name."

A viscous yellow-green blob launched from the third mouth. James jumped to the side, unsure about the nature of the attack. The liquid splattered against a boulder, sizzling and burning the top layers away.

"Acid, huh? Glad Shay was so obsessed with adapting me for that. That could have hurt." James reached for his holster and grunted. It was gone. It'd been burned to ashes, and his pistol was a half-melted mess yards away. "Fine. I'll do this the fun way."

The balaur stepped back and roared, its heads bobbing back and forth. It pushed off with its six legs, charging straight toward James, and the bounty-hunter-turned-dragon-slayer rushed to meet the monster. One of the three heads swung and smashed into him, sending him careening through the air.

James crashed to the ground with a grunt, the force of the blow more an inconvenience than painful, but his blade sank deep into the hard-packed soil. He stood and yanked it out of the ground.

"Better stick with the other shit, you three-headed asshole," James yelled. "I'm so adapted to kinetic attacks that I bet a fucking train could ram into me in advanced mode and I'd survive."

The monster roared again, the barking noise following.

James waited for another barrage of deadly breath, but none came. He wasn't sure if that meant the monster was holding back or if it took him a little while to regenerate the attacks.

"What are you?" came a deep bellowing voice from one of the heads.

Hey, it's English, or at least it sounds like it to me. That makes this shit easier.

"Oh, so you *can* talk," James replied. "I'm James Brownstone, a bounty hunter from LA. That means I take down dangerous fuckers for money. Fuckers like you."

"You aren't human," came a different but still low voice from another head. "You're barely hurt. You should be dead. I should be using your bones to clean my teeth."

"Yeah, a lot of people get confused by that. From what the lele tells me, you've killed a lot of people. It's too fucking bad they've closed this entire place off. I bet you would have made a nice level-five bounty, but she's paying me, so I'll still make some money out of this."

"You are arrogant, James Brownstone," the balaur

responded, this time from all three heads at the same time. "A creature can't win a battle merely by not dying. They have to kill their enemy. Your little sword arm won't get through my scales. I acknowledge that you are a worthy foe, but you are not a superior enemy."

"You really that confident, asshole?"

"I will leave this place today with your help," the balaur announced. "Your presence means there might be an opportunity to escape. Aid me, and you will be rewarded. Once I'm free of here, my power will be greater."

James pointed his blade at the center head. "How about I offer you another deal? I kill you, and the lele pays me."

The monster roared and stomped toward James. He didn't bother to dodge as the fire head clamped down on him. It lifted him as the acid head moved toward him.

Kill enemy, Whispy demanded.

"You breathe, James Brownstone," the balaur's acid head bellowed. "I have seen it. I will smother you. All creatures have weaknesses, and your arrogance has blinded you to yours. Then I will feast on your flesh to grow stronger."

James thrust his blade arm directly above him. The balaur roared in pain, and its mouth shot open. The bounty hunter fell to the ground, landing with a hard thud and a groan, the armor taking the impact.

He hopped to his feet and sprinted toward the creature's body. Another lighting ball exploded right behind him, and James dodged the follow-up acid attack. A small amount splashed on him and burned through his pants, but it didn't shave any layers off his armor.

James' charge ended with his blade impaling the front of the balaur. The creature roared and writhed as the bounty hunter jogged around the body, his weapon still embedded, and created a deep laceration extending from the front to the center of the body. A well-timed kick sent James rolling away, but blood spilled in a torrent from the wound, along with some muscle and what James took to be organs hanging out. It wasn't like he was an expert in magical zoology.

The creature bellowed and twitched, stumbling backward. "Brownstone!"

James growled and charged the balaur again, this time targeting the other side. The creature tried to kick his tormentor again, but his stiff moments allowed James to slice open the entire other side. The balaur collapsed to the ground, the roars from its three heads echoing in the nearby woods.

"I'll destroy you, Brownstone," the creature shrieked in unison. "You will suffer for this."

James leapt onto a leg and then atop the main torso. He ran toward the necks. A few quick hacks hewed through the neck of the acid head. The other two heads rushed toward him, and he removed the fire head from the body. The monster writhed in pain, a deep mournful groan issuing from the remaining mouth until James finished the removal of the last head. The body slumped.

An acrid stench seeped out of the necks.

James wrinkled his nose. "Fuck. That smell is deadlier than its damned breath."

All of James' wounds had healed by the time he returned to the pond, but that didn't do anything for his mostly missing clothes. If he didn't have his armor, he would be almost as naked as the lele. It was rare that he walked around in any stage of transformation for such a long time since normally he couldn't sustain the level of anger necessary to keep it going. It was an interesting experiment, and he liked having power on demand.

The lele stepped out of the pond as Brownstone approached, the diamond in her hand.

James imagined a shallow pocket in the side of his armor and it formed. He accepted the diamond and dropped it into the pocket. "Thanks. Now can you lead me to Shay, or is that going to be hard?"

The lele shook her head. "No, that task will be rather easy. Right now there's only one other human in this entire forest. Your woman." She started walking. "Let's go find her."

CHAPTER TWENTY-ONE

*Y*ou've got to be fucking kidding me, Shay thought as she lay on her stomach, peering over a small mound into the distance. The cobza raid had proven annoying enough, but she'd hoped that finding the instrument rather than recovering it would prove the primary issue.

The sight ahead of her let her know just how wrong she was.

Correk's damned chicken had led her to a single-story wooden fort infested with Zmeu. Dozens of the creatures were scattered around within the first zone of defense behind the seven-foot gated wooden fence.

How the hell did they even build this thing? I can see nearby stumps, so I get where they got the materials, but what did they use for tools? How did they plan it?

The Zmeu had proven to be far more industrious than she'd anticipated. Now she needed to figure the best way through them so she could get the instrument and rendezvous with James, wherever he was.

Some of the monsters stood or sat near firepits

roasting some sort of green-brown meat she didn't recognize. There was some barbeque she couldn't get behind.

A taller gate blocked Shay's view inside, but there was enough screeching and hissing to convince her there were probably dozens more inside the fort. She frowned at the chicken figurine on the ground beside her head. It was pointing straight at the fort.

Shay clung to the ridiculous hope that it might change for some reason, but it didn't. The cobza's location was clear, and while she didn't always trust that the Fixer's agenda would overlap with hers, the elf wasn't the kind of person who'd lead her and James into danger for the sake of a joke.

Makes sense that the cobza's there. The Zmeu must understand what it is and hope to use it somehow. All the more reason to get that thing out of there as quickly as possible.

A leaf crunched behind her, then another.

Shay whipped out her gun and rolled onto her back. She pointed the weapon behind her, ready to shoot whoever was coming. She relaxed as a familiar Los Angeles bounty hunter approached, and raised a curious eye at his companion.

James closed the distance between them until he was right in front of her. His body was mostly covered by his armor, but his pants were now more a loincloth rather than an article of clothing. The man being in his armor obviously post-fight wasn't surprising, but the smiling woman to his right was.

Okay, play it cool. Don't want to come off as a jealous harpy, but there's at least one question I have to ask.

Shay holstered her gun. "Why are you with some random naked chick? Who the hell is she?"

James shrugged. "She's a lele. She asked me to kill a balaur in exchange for a diamond and tracking you down."

"That actually makes a surprising amount of sense, considering where we are." Shay blinked. "Wait, did you say diamond?"

James reached into his pocket and pulled out a huge diamond as the lele beamed at Shay.

Since when does his armor have pockets?

Shay laughed. "Damn, you've been a busy beaver. I feel like a slacker in comparison." She nodded toward the lookout mound. "We've got a Zmeu fort over there, most likely with the cobza inside. I encountered a Zmeu earlier after we got separated. It wasn't a pleasant meeting."

"So did I." James grunted. "Already killed a bunch of them." He slapped a fist on his chest. "Fully adapted to their magic swords."

So that implies they got at least one good hit in. Those dragon men are tougher than I thought.

"I killed one, but he was really fucking obnoxious, so he should count for more than one." Shay shrugged.

"This situation no longer involves me," the lele stated with an annoyed look.

James nodded. "Thanks for your help."

"Thank you, James Brownstone, for clearing out the balaur." The lele offered a polite nod to Shay before sashaying off.

It took Shay a few seconds to recognize that the grass and brush she stepped over and around were slowly turning bright red.

"So now we have to deal with our fort," Shay commented. She pinched the bridge of her nose. "This shit has gotten complicated since the Zmeu decided they needed to show off their engineering skills. That's cute. Wonder who they're worried about, to make something like that. I doubt they just whipped up that thing in the last few hours because of you or me."

"There's a lot of angry and dangerous shit in this place." James shrugged. "I think we haven't seen half of it."

"Probably." Shay sighed. "You know, some days tomb raids don't bother me, and some days I find myself asking, 'What the hell is wrong with you, Shay? Why didn't you take up bartending?'"

James shrugged. "I hunt dangerous criminals. Not like shit's any better for me on most jobs. Even the low-level guys are mostly violent criminals."

Shay snickered. "Yeah, we've made questionable career choices, for sure." She shook her head. "But nothing we can do about that now. We need to get that cobza." She nodded in the general direction of the fort. "Probably over a hundred of our fine cannibal dragon-men friends manning the walls of Fort Annoyance over there."

"Are they technically cannibals? I mean, they eat people, but they aren't human." James furrowed his brow, thinking too much about the issue. "It's like feeding chicken to a parrot or something."

Shay pondered that for a few seconds before nodding. "Good point. Wait, does that mean if I ate an elf, I wouldn't be a cannibal?"

James stared at her with a confused expression. "Are you planning to eat an elf?"

"No, I just was..." Shay groaned. "Never mind. We'll worry about the nuances of cannibalism later. Let's concentrate on the assholes we have to kill right now. My sword worked well on the one I killed, but I didn't get a chance to test it on anyone else. You said you're adapted to them, which means they have enough power in their swords that they might be able to get through my defenses with enough effort."

James gestured to his chest. It took Shay a second to realize he was pointing to where his holster had once been.

Come to think of it, pretty much all his gear is gone, including his backpack. Did it all get destroyed?

Shay's backpack sat on the ground a yard away. She'd wanted to be ready to move rapidly.

"I tried shooting them with regular bullets, and it did jack shit," James explained. "Grenades also did shit." He raised his blade. "This went through them like they were made of paper."

Shay nodded. "So we're going to have to go in there and carve lizards up to get the cobza. I don't have enough anti-magic bullets on me to take out that many, so does a stabby-slashy plan sound good?"

"I don't think they can do much to me at this point. It'll just be a matter of how much fucking time it takes."

"Why? Got some special plans?" Shay grinned. "This recovery assumes you're not too busy running around with naked chicks. I didn't realize this tomb raid was going to turn into *Brownstone After Dark*. Might have packed a few extras for you. Special oils and shit."

James grunted. "It's not my fault she's naked. She's some

nymph thing. She did try to come onto me, and I told her to fuck off."

"When you get engaged to a woman, you're supposed to play the field less, not more." Shay winked, but the mirth left her face. "Your loyalty to me is the one thing I'll never question about you, James. Let me make that clear right now."

They stared at each other for a long moment.

Shay's face heated and she looked away. "Glad my plan worked, though."

"Plan?" James eyed her with suspicion. "What plan?"

"When I lost you through the miracle of what I assume was random portal shit, I decided to just go directly to the cobza under the theory that you'd eventually catch up, but I didn't expect you to become the Scourge of Zmeu and Saint Brownstone the Dragon Slayer in the meantime. You really did have a busy day, but at least now we know we have the resources we need to take down the little army gathered at Fort Annoyance."

"Oh, by the way, Whispy's figured how to feed the power to some of this shit off background magic." James shrugged, his bland expression not matching the huge revelation.

Shay blinked. "That's a pretty big damned deal. I was kind of wondering how you could be in advanced mode, because you don't seem pissed off at all."

"Not sure if it's gonna work in a place other than this, but at least it's let me stay in this form all day." James raised a blade and gave an evil grin. "I wonder about Oriceran. It's a good thing to test at some point in case I have to go fight more Drow."

Shay patted the hilt of her sword. "Maybe we can convince the Zmeu to surrender the cobza, considering all the noise you've been making. A victory by force of will rather than random slaughter might be nice."

James marched toward the lookout.

"Where are you going?" Shay asked.

"To talk to them. Might as well get this shit over with." James shrugged. "Not like I'm getting anything else out of fighting the fuckers at this point."

"So much for even considering a surprise attack." Shay jogged after him. "When I said maybe we could convince them, that was just a suggestion. I thought we were going to go through a few more options."

"It's a good plan, so why spend more time talking?" James jumped off the short lip of the hill. Screeches and hisses erupted from the Zmeu behind the fence, along with other noise from inside the stronghold. The enemy had eyes on them.

"I'm James Brownstone," the bounty hunter bellowed, his voice carrying. "I'm here with a woman to get the cobza you've got in there." He continued his advance. "If you're thinking, 'We'll just fight this guy and eat him,' you should know I've already killed a shitload of you, as well as a balaur. To be honest, I want to kill you scaly motherfuckers because you eat people, but I figure at some point they're gonna figure out how to fix all the shit around here and then the Romanian government will probably bomb the fuck out of you anyway." He shrugged. "Why waste my time? But let's make this shit clear: If you fight us, you will die. If you leave right now, you won't. Or if you give us the cobza, we walk away and you get to live for at least one more day, but any choice involving fighting us will end with you dead."

"Nice intimidation," Shay observed.

Angry screeches followed, along with so many hisses it sounded like a river for a moment. The Zmeu summoned their dark blades out of smoke, enough that a billowing cloud spread above the fort. Faint hints of sulfur filtered from it.

Wonder if that means they're demons? Or maybe something else. Who the fuck knows?

"It doesn't seem like they're getting scared," Shay observed, lowering her hand to her sword. "And no one's calling back in English. Looks like it's going to be the hard way. Well, you gave them a chance to surrender. Not our fault they're choosing to get sliced up."

"This is what happens when you don't pay attention to your local news." James shrugged. He jogged toward the fence. "Let's just clear them out and get this over with. I want to get the fuck out of this forest."

Shay headed after her man, not yet drawing her *tachi*. She wanted to wait until she was closer so as not to waste energy.

I wonder what it would have been like to have James with me on all my longer tomb raids. Like that shit in Australia.

The Zmeu continued to screech and hiss while rhythmically banging their swords against the ground or fence. James continued toward the large wooden gate securing the front fence. Several of the dragon men rushed toward it, ready to intercept the armored bounty hunter and the tomb raider.

Shay and James closed to twenty yards.

"Ready?" James asked. "I'm gonna do this the direct way. No fancy shit, since they can't hurt me."

"You do what you need to," Shay replied. "I'll clean up afterward."

With a grunt, James broke into a sprint and barreled toward the gate. Shay picked up her pace but didn't match his. Even with the pendant and the ring, it made more sense to let James take the lead and bear the brunt of the enemy's attention.

He smashed shoulder-first into the gate with an echoing crash. One of the wooden doors ripped off its hinges and collapsed on the Zmeu on the other side. A river of dark swords and green scales surged toward the opening and the invader.

Here we go.

James recovered quickly and swung his blade in a wide arc, and a whole line of the enemy fell to the ground in a bloody heap. Other Zmeu slashed at James or tried to bite or claw him, but their attacks accomplished nothing more than setting the creatures up for easy counterattacks from the armored bounty hunter.

The enemies bodies began to pile up as the writhing mass of reptilian monsters surrounded James, every individual creature desperately seeking a weak spot.

Their focus on James gave Shay her opening. She arrived at the entrance and started slashing with wild abandon. The *tachi* cut deep into the flesh of the Zmeu. Her initial victim lost his head, just as the first Zmeu she'd encountered had. The next several dropped as she pierced their chests or slashed at their legs.

With a roar, James threw several of the monsters off

him. His follow-up thrusts came so quickly it was almost mechanical, with a new enemy dead every second. The Zmeu apparently refused to believe they couldn't overwhelm their nemesis with sheer numbers as they continued to hack away at him, but even the lucky few who struck his non-armored neck or head were surprised that they netted only quickly healing scratches.

There's brave, and then there's stupid.

The initial dozens of foes dropped to a single dozen after a few minutes and were reduced to a half-dozen a minute later. The last Zmeu in the outer yard fell to Shay's blade.

Shay took short, ragged breaths as she walked through the tangled pile of dead monsters toward James, who had been painted blue by the enemy's blood. She pushed a body out of the way with her foot. "That was some old-fashioned ultra-violence." She nodded toward the inner gate. "Maybe that convinced them of the wisdom of diplomatic solutions."

James turned toward the inner gate and raised his blade. "Give us the cobza or die, assholes."

"That's pretty straightforward, but these things have come off so far as pretty stubborn. Here's hoping." Shay frowned and grabbed a rag out of her bag to wipe the Zmeu blood off her blade.

"If they're smart enough to build a fort then they're worried about survival," James replied, his low voice reminding her of an avalanche. "That means we can reason with them, and they just saw half their guys get taken out. Not everyone is as dumb as the Harriken."

The inner gates squeaked open. Zmeu were shoulder to

shoulder inside, their swords at the ready. There was a commotion at the back and some sort of undulating movement through the crowd. They were passing a cloth sack to the front.

The sack finally reached the front Zmeu, and the monsters tossed it in front of the gate before several of them scrambled to pull the inner gate doors closed again. A loud, resounding *thunk* followed as they secured the door.

James could get through that. Hell, I could.

James jogged over and picked up the bag, then opened it and pulled out a musical instrument with a two-tone wooden body. Despite being hundreds of years old, the varnish gleamed like new under the sunlight streaming through the trees around them.

"What do you know?" Shay smiled. "Sometimes people learn their lesson, or at least dragon-men do."

James tossed the instrument back in the bag. "There's hope for the fucking world yet. You still have the tracker to get us back to the car, or will I need to cut more naked-chick deals?"

"I've got the tracker." Shay sheathed her sword. "No more naked chicks today for you besides me."

CHAPTER TWENTY-TWO

Trey parked his truck across the street from the huge gated mansion, his phone to his ear. "You got the address, Vic?"

"Yes," Victoria responded. "I still think you should have let me come. You didn't mention earlier that you were walking straight into Paul Esposito's mansion. I was thinking this was going to be you meeting someone at a restaurant, not you going into a Mafia don's house by yourself."

"I don't even know if this shit has anything to do with him or if this is just where they wanted me."

Trey was suspicious of the entire situation, given that Paul's son had tried to forge an alliance with the agency through him not all that long before, but pushing too hard the opposite direction risked causing trouble. He still wasn't sure why he was there or who he was meeting, but he assumed this was just a flashier effort by Marco Esposito to convince Trey of the importance of a Brownstone-Esposito pact.

"I didn't know where I was going until I checked the address." Trey snorted. "Besides, sometimes it's about making a statement, and the Families understand and respect statements."

"And what statement are you making?"

Trey turned his engine off. "That the Brownstone Agency ain't afraid of no one. Besides, if this was about wasting my ass, they would have already taken the chance. They had to know that even if I didn't bring no one here, I'd be telling people. And with James' rep, if I disappear inside some mobster's mansion, he'd be kicking the door in the next day and demanding to know where the fuck I was."

"That's true," Victoria replied. "But make sure you're wearing your gloves in case this turns into a shitstorm. All you have to do is make it out of there if it turns into one."

Trey glanced down at his already-gloved hands with a grin. "I'll make sure to do that. If I don't give you a call in an hour, come a-knockin' with the boys."

Victoria chuckled darkly. "Yeah, that will send a message. Talk to you soon."

Trey ended the call. He slipped the phone back into his pocket, stepped out of his truck, and walked over to the gate. Bright lights lit up the vast lawn, and a single huge multi-tier fountain lay in the center.

I wonder if I'm being a dumb motherfucker about this. Maybe the Mafia wants to make a statement by taking me out.

Trey snorted. If they did, the Espositos, if not all the local Families, would end up joining the Harriken in hell.

He looked for a callbox, but the gate rumbled and opened.

"Looks like an invitation to me." Trey adjusted his tie and smoothed his lapels, then slipped through the gate and onto the marble walkway. Small lights lining the walkway on either side illuminated the path that led up to and around both sides of the fountain before ending at the front door.

The Espositos maintained a nice lawn and fountain. Trey would give them that, even if they seemed allergic to the idea of having any trees around.

He checked around for any obvious snipers but saw no one. When he'd passed the fountain, the front door opened. Marco, along with several other men, stepped outside with polite smiles on their faces. They might have guns on them, but they didn't have them out.

Not like they'd cap my ass outside where some drone could take pictures of them. There are statements, and then there's just being a dumb motherfucker.

Trey arrived at the porch and gave Marco a polite nod. "What's up, Marco?"

Just me meeting a bunch of mobsters like it ain't no thing.

"I'm glad you could join us, Trey," Marco responded. "I wanted to personally deliver the invitation earlier, but I was taking care of some Family business."

Trey gestured toward the house. "Why all the big mystery and shit? When I was asking earlier, your guys wouldn't tell me."

"That's my father's doing. He likes to mess with people's heads." Marco grinned. "I hope you're not too pissed."

So this is about Paul Esposito, huh?

Trey shrugged. "I'm here, ain't I?"

Marco opened the door and motioned Trey inside.

"You'll be meeting with my father." He held out his hand. "I'm afraid I'm going to have to ask you to give me your gun. That's another rule of my father's. Only Family can keep their guns around him."

Trey pulled out his gun and handed it to Marco. The mobster's gaze rested on Trey's gloved hands for a moment and a questioning expression spread over his face.

"I gave you my *gun,*" Trey emphasized. "That don't mean I'm gonna do whatever you ask. *You* asked *me* to show up, not the other damned way around." He removed the gloves and slipped them into his pocket. "But it's not cold inside."

"No, it isn't." Marco handed the weapon to one of the others.

"Let's go meet Daddy Esposito," Trey replied with a grin, even though his heart rate had kicked up. An ambush might be able to take him if he didn't have his gloves on. He didn't know if he was being brave or an idiot like so many of the arrogant bounties he'd taken down throughout the years.

Just got to trust my instincts and training—but I'm taking at least one fucker with me if they try any shit.

Marco chuckled and led Trey inside and down a vase- and statue-filled hallway with an arched ceiling. The hallway led directly to a vast living room. A dapper white-haired man in a sports coat waited in the palatial space.

Trey recognized him instantly, as would anyone with even the most casual of connection to the Vegas underworld. It was Paul Esposito.

Here we go.

The Mafia don nodded toward a chair near him. He looked at Marco. "I'll call if I need you."

The other mobsters departed the room.

Doubt he's gonna cap my ass with all his guys out of the room.

Trey walked over to the indicated chair and took a seat, then folded his hands in his lap and inhaled deeply. This was one time he truly needed Smooth Trey, even if it was annoying to go against his deeply-ingrained speech patterns. He suspected that Paul Esposito would respond to him more positively if he changed the way he talked.

"Trey Garfield," Paul commented. "It's a pleasure to meet you. I've heard a lot about you." He looked Trey up and down. "You're better dressed than a lot of my guys."

"It's nice to meet you as well," Trey replied with a grin. "And I do try to look good, but let's say this was a big surprise to me. I didn't expect to get an invitation to meet with you this morning when I got up. I thought your guys had come to kill my ass."

Paul let out a hearty laugh. "Sorry about that. I would have thought the same thing. Mostly I just wanted to give you time to think about it and see how you'd react." He waved a hand. "I've looked into you, you know. Your past, and how you grew up; the gang you were in. I know all about you. You could say I'm a big fan. I came up hard too, and I made something of myself despite people trying to hold me back."

What the fuck is all this supposed to mean? Is this mother-fucker trying to threaten me, or is he trying to convince me we're the same kind of man? Better make some shit clear before he gets the wrong idea.

Trey cleared his throat. "I should tell you, Mr. Esposito, that I spoke to your son about his earlier offer. I thought I made our position clear, and the answer I gave him represents the official position of the Brownstone Agency. If you got the big man himself to show up, he'd say the same thing."

"That's not what this is about." Paul shook his head. "And I'd rather not be in the same room as James Brownstone...ever. I respect his power, but to me, it'd be like being in the same room as a tiger, or even a tornado."

"He *is* a pretty intense man." Trey shrugged. "If this ai... isn't about an alliance, then what is it about?"

"Don't worry about that. The past is the past, and I understand why you feel the way you do. Quite frankly, your position is fair." Paul furrowed his brow. "And after what happened to the Harriken, I think everyone in a business like ours understands that sometimes there will be sacrifices if the wrong choices are made." He chuckled. "You're too young to remember how different it was, let alone here."

"Different?" Trey frowned. "What are you talking about?"

"The Mafia was dying in Vegas, especially the Italian Mafia. The Feds had ripped our balls off through the decades, and more vicious groups were cutting into our territory from the opposite side." The Mafia leader shook his head, faint disgust on his face. "There were still Families, and they had influence, but it wasn't like the golden days. Then all that shit with Oriceran happened, and everything changed. Opportunities arose, and those who took advantage of those opportunities did well." He smiled. "That's what success in life is about: flexibility. That's why you are doing well. Let's face it, you were dealt a shit hand, growing up in that neighborhood, but you saw an opportunity in the gang. You followed it up, and then Brownstone gave you another opportunity, and you took it.

"That's why I like you. Because you're the kind of man who seizes on an opportunity to improve himself regardless of the situation."

Despite what he just said, it sounds like this motherfucker's buttering me up to ask for an alliance again. What, he thinks if he just says how smart I am, I'll roll over and let him pat my belly?

Trey's gaze cut around the room. Paul really liked old paintings. Art appreciation was still fairly low on the things Trey cared about.

"I like to think I'm not a dumbass," Trey explained. "But I've made plenty of mistakes in my life, and I'll make plenty more. Fortunately, I was given chances. Opportunities, like you said."

"Yes, you were given some chances, or at least, one big chance." Paul leaned back and inhaled deeply. "Mercy's a good thing, don't you think? I was wondering how things would have been different if Brownstone was more like the Silver Ghost."

Trey's face tightened. His and Victoria's thorough ass-kicking at the Silver Ghost's hands still rubbed him raw months later. It didn't matter that she was dead.

He asked, "You mean if the big man was a crazy vigilante?"

Paul nodded. "Yes. I've seen the kind of things he can

do. He could have killed or maimed every single person in your gang to get you out of his neighborhood."

"Sure, but we always showed him proper respect. James Brownstone understands respect, just like y'all."

"That's good to hear." Paul rubbed his chin. "And you agree on the importance of mercy?"

"Yeah, of course." Trey nodded. "That's the way the Brownstone Agency works. A lot of times if it's a low-level guy, we try to get them to surrender so no one has to get hurt, bounty or bounty hunter. We try to keep our guys under control. Our hope is that our combination of reputation for being badasses as well as professionals who don't hurt people just for the sake of hurting people will lead to fewer confrontations. I can't say it always works, but I think it's helpful."

"It's a good strategy." Paul raised his leg and rested his foot on his knee. "And that mercy and restraint are what I wanted to talk to you about."

"Yeah?"

"The other day you picked up a bounty, Gino Cantu," Paul began.

Okay, here we go. He's all smiles, but he's pissed that the fucker got picked up.

Trey lifted his chin. "I did, at that. Level two. I understand he's had some dealings with the Mafia, including the Espositos, but he had a valid bounty. I took him down based on that. Brownstone Agency doesn't go after people without bounties unless they come after us."

Paul's affable smile turned into a frown. "My understanding is that there was an incident during the apprehension. An extreme incident."

"Another bounty hunter not affiliated with the Brownstone Agency showed up. He initiated his recovery attempt with a grenade. I won't apologize for that dumbass motherfucker. I beat his ass down for multiple reasons, including the fact that he threw a motherfucking grenade near me."

Trey assumed that the mobster could handle his normal speech patterns. If you couldn't call a man a motherfucker for throwing a grenade right next to you, when could you?

Paul shook a finger. "Yes, I heard how you beat the guy up, and that was what I was curious about. So you were just mad about the grenade, then? Or was it more about him trying to jump your bounty? I know your type can get territorial."

Trying to figure out which bounty hunter to be pissed at, Esposito?

Trey scoffed. "I'm not gonna lie. I was angry about that shit, too, but that wasn't the main thing that got my fists flying. I don't know all the details of why, but there was a kid there. I didn't like the idea of some motherfucker throwing grenades around when there was a kid who could have taken shrapnel. Cantu might have picked his lifestyle and accepted the risk, but that kid didn't. A little restraint wouldn't hurt, so I helped the other bounty hunter understand that."

Paul blew out a breath and smacked his lips. "No hurting kids. That's a good policy. It's how we operate, too. No kids. No wives. Not all Families have those policies, but I think there are some lines that shouldn't be crossed. It's the difference between being a businessman and being a thug. The world doesn't need more thugs."

"I agree, Mr. Esposito."

I don't get his angle in all this. I thought he was gonna be pissed about Cantu, but he don't seem to give a shit. Maybe he just figures Jared's the one who should get fucked up over it.

"I'm going to tell you something that very few people in this area know, Trey." Paul stared at him gravely. "It's going to come out very soon anyway, and I want you to understand how important what happened the other day was."

Trey frowned, now even more confused.

"Gino Cantu is my son," Paul explained. "His mom was a waitress at a club I was running back in the day. We had some fun times between the sheets, but it was nothing serious. Then I found out she was knocked up. I told her I couldn't acknowledge the kid." He looked uncomfortable. "My dearly departed wife, God rest her soul, would have never forgiven me, but I made sure he was taken care of, and when the time came a few years back, I made sure he had opportunities to get involved with the family business. But I had to be careful." He frowned. "Very few people know who Gino actually is. Even he didn't know for most of his life. It was something his mom agreed to a long time ago. Originally, it was to keep them safe, and after that it was just because he didn't know, and it was too much a dick move to come in years later and say, 'Hey, I'm your dad.' I let him know the truth recently, and we're trying to understand each other better. Soon I'm going to let everyone know, which is why I feel comfortable telling you."

Trey blinked as he processed the information. "I guess it was a good thing that I didn't rough up Gino, then. But you got to understand, it is Brownstone policy. I didn't have a clue who he was."

"That doesn't matter." Paul threaded his fingers together. "And that little boy you were so concerned about is my grandson." His face darkened. "If the other bounty hunter had hurt him, I would have made him pay, but it wouldn't have mattered. Decades in this business have taught me that revenge doesn't bring anyone back."

"Shit." Trey blinked. "Damn."

"Exactly. Your restraint was not only respectful of my Family, but I heard how you threw yourself on Gino. Your fancy magic might have saved him from getting killed, and if you had not taken on that other bounty hunter, my grandson might have been hurt, or worse." Paul smiled. "So, no, if Gino had to be taken down on a bounty, I'm glad it was by you, Trey.

"But here's the thing. As far as I'm concerned, I owe you a favor. A big favor, and I'm a man who always pays his favors."

Trey shook his head. "I don't know about that. I was just doing my job. The Brownstone Agency strives to be something more than a bunch of thugs, you know what I'm saying? Bounty hunters; no more, no less."

"Just think about it," Paul replied. "And no matter what you say, I owe you a favor. Family men always pay their debts, and I'm sure you can find a use for it at some point in the future." He chuckled. "And don't worry. I understand this doesn't change anything between the Esposito Family or any other Mafia Family and the Brownstone Agency." He glanced at his watch. "But I'm sorry. I have to wrap this up. I've got meetings I need to go to, but I thought it was important that I talk to you face-to-face about this."

Trey just stared at the mob boss, at a rare loss for words. Finally, he managed to open his mouth. "Thanks."

Damn. This is some shit I never thought would happen today.

CHAPTER TWENTY-THREE

It's good to be back home, James thought. *No weird-ass monsters. No crazy forests. No walled-in shit patrolled by soldiers. Tomb raiding leads to weird places. It's probably a good thing that Shay's dialing that shit down.*

He put up the footrest on his recliner. He liked having his dog sitting at his feet. Mack was always great when it came to dog watching, but flying to a foreign country to deal with a weird magical anarchy zone had been annoying.

At least the Professor has the stupid instrument and can stick it in whatever big hole he takes all the dangerous artifacts. I wonder if he blows up shit like the cobza or sends it to the World in Between, or just tosses it in some landfill in Iowa.

James grunted and decided that the less he knew, the better.

Shay's right, though. If I can travel to places like Romania, I can go to other places. It might not hurt to hit high-level bounties around the world more often. Not like I've never done that. Bounty-hunting road trip or some shit like that.

Shay emerged from the bedroom in a robe, her hair up in a towel, droplets of water still on her face from her shower. "I meant to tell you before I got in the shower that I was catching up on important shit on my phone and found out there's a bridal show at the Convention Center. I was thinking about us going to that. All sorts of vendors and ideas. Not just regular stuff, magical shit, too."

James shook his head. "No fucking way. The flower shop was bad enough. How many fucking shades of pink did that guy claim there were? They all looked exactly the same. Besides, if you're gonna do boring shit like that, just hire a wedding planner."

Shay sighed. "I'm trying to generate a bunch of ideas before I worry about committing to anything or anyone, but if you don't want to go, that's fine. I won't force you."

"Jessie Rae's and Father McCartney," James reiterated. "That's non-negotiable. You can have thirty-four fucking shades of pink if you want."

"Duly noted and remembered." Shay put her hands on her hips. "Do *you* believe I'm going to have thirty-four shades of pink at my wedding?"

"Probably not."

"Exactly. For now, though, I'm going to go get dressed so I can go to the bridal show...by myself." Shay winked and headed back into the bedroom.

Huh. Speaking of important shit, maybe I should see what's up too. The only interesting bounty anyone's mentioned was Trey telling me about that mobster.

James pulled his phone out of his pocket and brought up the bounty hunting app. He sorted for level four and above bounties, with a filter for Los Angeles County. Nothing came up.

Huh. The agency can handle everything else. Guess the big boys are quiet right now.

He was just about to turn his phone off when the app beeped with a new bounty alert that fit his parameters. He tapped on it, a slight smile on his face. It'd been a while since a level five had hit LA.

"Let's see what we've got."

A NEW LEVEL FIVE BOUNTY HAS BEEN ISSUED BY THE LOS ANGELES POLICE DEPARTMENT. IT IS FUNDED BY THE CITY OF LOS ANGELES, COUNTY OF LOS ANGELES, AND CITY OF PROVIDENCE, RHODE ISLAND.

Officially released information on LYLE LASSOM as follows:

James scrolled down to a security camera picture of an unassuming brown-haired man. The man's appearance did not scream badass in even the remotest sense of the word.

Huh. He must have super-powerful magic or some shit. Hope he's not a necromancer. Motherfucking zombies.

LYLE LASSOM, 25-year-old Caucasian male, is responsible for two homicides in the city of Providence, Rhode Island, and multiple homicides in the city of Los Angeles in connection with the Sherman Oaks explosion and other unrelated incidents. Suspect is also responsible for other crimes, including but not limited to inciting to riot, grand theft, grand theft auto, kidnapping, illegal smuggling of artifacts, violation of FAA Hazardous Materials regulations, resisting arrest, and assaulting a law enforcement officer.

LYLE LASSOM's whereabouts are unknown at this time, but he is currently believed to be operating in Los Angeles County.

Abilities channeled via magical artifact described as BONE CHARM NECKLACE include extreme mental manipulation and/or control manifesting as oral orders to humanoid subjects which they blindly follow. Note that such orders can lead to direct harm of self and others, including possible forced suicide.

This is classified as a LEVEL FIVE bounty at this time. Appropriate licensing is required for recovery of the bounty.

Please be advised this is a FULL LIVE recovery bounty. Termination of the bounty will result in forfeiting 100% of the pre-tax value of the bounty.

All licensed bounty hunters attempting to capture the bounty should exercise extreme caution and assume the bounty may possess additional weapons or abilities not specified in this notice. These additional abilities may result in a more difficult bounty hunting experience than suggested by the current bounty level.

The City of Los Angeles and the City of Los Angeles Police Department are not responsible for any death, injury, or loss of property that occurs as a result of pursuing LYLE LASSOM. Incidental damage or injury of third-parties will be the legal responsibility of the bounty hunter, not the city of Los Angeles or the City of Los Angeles Police Department.

Please note that all bounties are subject to the State of California Bounty Hunting Tax and Federal income taxes. Appropriate reporting forms will be sent to the

IRS and California Department of Taxation and Fee Administration following award of the bounty.

Click here for additional information, including further legal disclaimers.

James grunted. High-level bounties without nicknames were always the most dangerous. Those kinds of men didn't have anything to prove. The non-badass picture was more proof. This Lassom might be one of the more dangerous men to ever come to Los Angeles.

He headed to the bedroom. Shay sat on the bed doing her makeup with the aid of a compact.

"A level-five bounty just popped up," James told her. "I'm gonna check into it."

Shay looked up. "Right now? You just got back last night from helping me on the tomb raid."

"Yeah." James frowned. "I don't like the look of this guy. They say he can get into people's heads."

"Did you need my help? If it's a level five, it might require the engagement jewelry and *tachi* combo to help you out."

James shook his head. "Not right away. I've got to check on some shit first. I have no idea where the asshole even is."

Shay nodded. "All right, but call me if you need my help."

Shit, both Peyton and Heather are on vacation. How am I gonna track this guy down easily? Guess it's time to pay the man a visit.

Several heads turned as James threw open the door to the Black Sun and entered. He took a few steps inside, lingering by a table just to see the gang member there twitch a little.

Good. I'll respect this place's neutrality, but I want all you assholes to remember I'm around.

James headed to Tyler at the bar and gestured at the hall leading to Tyler's office. "We need to talk. Now."

The information broker's face tightened, and he leaned over to whisper something to the other bartender. The young woman, a new hire, nodded quickly.

James didn't wait before heading into the hallway. He leaned against the wall by the door to Tyler's office.

The information broker turned the corner with a deep frown. He threw open the door to his office and stomped in, his face red and pinched with anger.

"You can't just come into my place and snap your fingers, Brownstone," Tyler bitched as he dropped into his desk chair. "It makes me look bad. It makes me look like a pussy. Yeah, yeah, you could kick me to the moon, but you don't need to disrespect me in my own place."

"Sorry." James entered the office and closed the door. "This is high-priority and I'm down some resources, so I need your help to take care of a bounty."

"What could be such a high priority..." Tyler made a face. "It's Lyle Lassom, isn't it? I knew the minute I saw that bounty notice that you'd be rushing right after the little hypnofreak."

James crossed his arms. "Don't tell me you don't know where he is. Everybody's been talking about how you've picked up a lot of the slack from the Eyes. Fuck, some people even say I killed the Eyes for you just so you could do that."

Tyler sighed. "Here's the problem. You know how it is. If it's a low-level bounty, that's one thing, but me giving up information on a level-five bounty is asking for them to come after me, and this guy's even scarier than you."

"Scarier than *me*?" James growled.

"Yes! Did you read the information in the bounty notice? He was nothing just a couple of weeks ago, and he's already a level five. He can make someone kill themselves by just telling them to do it. This guy finds out I helped you and comes here, I'm dead, and he'll probably make me do the killing. Or he'll make me hurt my employees or Maria." Tyler grimaced. "The PDA's all over this too, but they can't track him directly because of something related to the necklace he uses for his power."

"I didn't ask if someone else could track him. I asked if you knew where he was." James frowned. "And if this fucker's so dangerous, that's all the more reason to give him up. Every minute he's free, he can mindfuck someone new. I'm gonna find him eventually one way or another. This way, you help me ensure he's not fucking more people over in the meantime."

Tyler stared at James like he was an idiot. "You haven't thought this through, have you?"

"Yeah, I have. Step one, find the guy. Step two, kick the guy through a window. Step three, collect the bounty."

Tyler groaned. "Here's the problem, Brownstone. You're the toughest badass in America. No one's going to question that, and I've made a lot of money with my 'always bet on Brownstone' policy, but this is one enemy who isn't tough. You can't beat him by being the tougher guy." He took a deep breath and slowly let it out. "Don't you get it? He's not a badass. He controls people's minds. If I send you to this guy and he takes over your mind, what happens, huh? You think of that? What if he sends you downtown and tells you to kill everyone you possibly can?"

James grunted. "Everything you're telling me only makes me want to take him down more, and I'm not so easy to mind control. I've fought these things called despair bugs that get in your head, and I beat them."

Tyler scoffed. "So, I'm supposed to risk Los Angeles—and my damned life, by the way—because you're cocky enough to think you can win against this guy? There's being strong-willed, and then there's magic. Did you read about the wizards in Providence? Two powerful wizards and he had them kill each other with their powers. That means the magic's not limited to simple actions or whatever. He'll get in your head, Brownstone."

"I've also got anti-magic deflectors." James frowned. "And how is it risking *your* life?"

"The first thing the guy will probably ask you is, 'Who told you where I am?'" Tyler threw up his hands in frustration. "Not only do I not want Lassom showing up and telling me to literally fuck myself before I kill myself, the word on the street is that the guy's already snagged some major magical talent as bodyguards. And that's not even the worst part."

"What's the worst part?" James asked.

Tyler narrowed his eyes. "You haven't checked in with the cops yet on this, have you?"

"No, I came straight here. I need to find the guy before I

can think about how I'm gonna take him down."

"Lassom's been moving around a lot, but he's worried about the cops and the feds, so from what I've heard, he's grabbed tons of random-ass people off the street and used his mind control on them to turn them into security. They're human shields to slow down the cops." Tyler rubbed his temples. "You see what I'm getting at, Brownstone? You can't solve this the way you solve everything else. You can't just storm in there and punch most of them through the wall and gun down the others. You can't win against this guy because you can't even get near him. To win against someone like this, you'd need a backup brain."

"Or I could use an anti-magic deflector and finish him quickly."

"And if you lose the deflector? What then?"

"I've got other tricks." James lowered his arms to his sides. "If we wait too long on this it's only going to get worse. He already blew up half a block. What if he decides it's funny to mind-control a SWAT team? No, fuck this guy. Give him up, and I'll handle him."

Tyler sneered. "Do you think everyone's still going to like you after they find out you killed a bunch of innocent people who were mind-controlled? Do you think the cops will? Because that's what you're talking about here, Brownstone. You're talking about taking on a man who mostly is using innocent people to protect himself. If you're not damn careful, you'll end up killing someone innocent."

James grunted. As much as he hated to admit it, Tyler had a point. The Brownstone strategy typically relied on overwhelming physical force to either directly defeat an enemy or awe them into submission. He'd beaten the balaur by charging in and cutting it open, and the Zmeu through brutal direct attacks. Those kinds of tactics in the current situation would leave him with a higher innocent body count than the bounty already had.

"All I have to do is not kill everyone." James scratched his chin. "I can do that."

"Can you not kill everyone when a bunch of people are trying to kill you?" Tyler shook his head. "Including magicals? Sit this one out, Brownstone. Let the government handle it."

James chuckled. "No, I won't wait. I've got a plan, and it'll help make sure that no innocent people get seriously hurt, but the plan requires you to tell me where Lassom is."

"Maybe I don't know. It's not like he called me up and introduced himself."

The men locked eyes. Tyler gritted his teeth, his hands pressed so hard to his desk his knuckles turned white.

"Fine." Tyler yanked out his phone and tapped in a text to James. "I've just sent you the address. The guy's latest digs are in some office he stole from a bunch of lawyers. Normally, I'd say it was poetic justice, but this Lassom guy freaks me out almost as much as the Eyes. At least the Eyes had the excuse of being a batshit-crazy gnome. This guy is just some punk who got his hands on power."

James' phone buzzed a few seconds later and he gave Tyler a tight smile. "Well, I killed the Eyes, so there's no reason I can't take down Lassom, too. Thanks, Tyler." He stood and texted Shay.

Gonna need you. I'll call you in 15 minutes to explain the details. Have to make a few other calls first to set some shit up.

CHAPTER TWENTY-FOUR

James stepped out the back door of the Brownstone building to take a look at the gathered field employees. His black-suited bounty hunters were all geared up in bulletproof vests and the primary equipment they'd need for the job: stun rifles, stun rods, and sonic grenades. Everyone also had a handgun with anti-magic bullets that they were to use only if there was no other choice. It wasn't every Brownstone Agency bounty hunter, since a small team, including Trey and Victoria, were still in Vegas, but it was every other man or woman who wasn't sick.

Damn. I do *have an army.*

There were anti-magic deflectors available for only half the bounty hunters, so they had been broken into teams of one bounty hunter with a deflector and another without. The deflector team members were to monitor each other in case someone showed signs of mind control, and the personnel without a deflector wouldn't be sweeping deep into the target building.

If James' plan worked, the only people going very far into the building would be him and Shay.

We've got the people and the coordination. Lassom has that charm, but he was just a piece-of-shit nobody before, which means he doesn't know how to use his magic to its maximum potential. We can win this and make sure that asshole rots in a cell where he has no control.

Shay leaned against the wall near the door, her arms crossed and a nonchalant look on her face. She had her defensive artifacts ready, and a stun rifle slung over her shoulder, but no sword. Her gnome-crafted knives and gun were in their sheaths and holster on her tactical vest, but James hoped they would only have to come out at the end.

Maria stepped in front of the gathered crowd. "Listen up. James has the location of this Lyle Lassom, and initial drone recon suggests a heavy armed presence inside the building. We can't assume that anyone we encounter is doing so freely so this will be a non-lethal sweep, just like we've done before. Consider all those criminals you didn't care about practice for these civilians."

James grunted and stood beside Maria. "From what my informant has told me, there will be high-level threats present. Don't bother with them if you encounter them. You leave them to me. Concentrate on taking everyone else down without killing them. We're going in force to end this shit quickly and ensure Lassom doesn't get away."

"AET has been contacted," Maria explained. "They will be coordinating their efforts with ours."

"The cops are letting a bunch of bounty hunters take point?" Lachlan asked, shaking his head. "That's new shit."

"Not really." Maria shrugged. "When Brownstone took

down the Harriken, it was a similar situation. Sometimes a bounty hunter might have better resources. Besides, in this case, the AET doesn't have enough personnel to success-fully secure the location on their own, especially when the main group of enemy gunmen might really be innocent civilians."

Ethan frowned from the crowd. "Not a lot of AET, but what about SWAT or just regular cops?"

Maria shook her head. "It's too dangerous to send in regular SWAT or officers since they'll be vulnerable to Lassom's magic. The AET are the only cops in the depart-ment with access to anti-magic deflectors. They send in a SWAT team, that SWAT team will open fire on other cops a few moments later. I'm being blunt. There's no fucking way the Chief of Police will allow any situation that looks like it might end in blue-on-blue fatalities, and he's got our agency to help ensure that doesn't happen." She cut through the air with her hand. "Don't let the civilians being involved part freak you out. This is simple shit, people. We've breached and cleared with complete non-lethal clearance before even without James, and this time, we have him with us."

James nodded once.

She scoffed. "There's a reason that level fours and fives avoid this city, and that reason is James Brownstone. Today we're going to send a message to every piece-of-shit high-level threat in this country that it's not just James Brown-stone they have to be afraid of, but every single bounty hunter in his agency.

"Now, let's go take down a level five."

The bounty hunters roared their approval.

Shay grinned. "I'm starting to let myself get excited."

Multiple AET drones flew overhead, focused on the exterior of the two-story office building. A small AET strike team was on standby in a helicopter in case Lassom ran. The other AET forces were deployed along the back of the office building to seal the exits. James and his team stomped toward the front door as soon as the police were in position.

The intimidating black-suited army of the Brownstone Agency marched in lockstep, their stun rifles in hand and their faces set in grim determination.

In truth, James wasn't going to make much money on the bounty. Spreading it around to almost the entire agency meant the relative value for each individual was low, and he was kicking in for bonuses out of his pocket on top of that, but he couldn't stand by while someone like Lyle Lassom was fucking with his city.

Most criminals were parasites, and good parasites knew not to kill the host. Lassom wasn't a parasite. He was a cancer who would spread unless he was excised right now.

Moderate adaptation potential, Whispy Doom estimated

James had bonded the symbiont before arrival. The more James thought about what Lyle had done—stripping away people's free will and making them do horrible things—the more pissed he got. Even Satan gave people a choice. The little prick needed to pay, but still, the boiling rage that only came with direct threats to his family didn't wash through James.

Is there enough power for advanced transformation? James asked.

Limited alternative power available for advanced transformation, Whispy responded. *Sustained operation may not be possible.*

So there it was. There wasn't enough background magic in a normal Earth city to freely borrow power for his most powerful mode, but it was still good to know he could call it on command for a short period if needed.

For the moment, though, he was relying on his amulet's basic hardening, interface, and regeneration capabilities. Lassom might not be tough, but if he had deadly wizards with him, things might get challenging.

Shay frowned and held up the clear crystal hanging around her neck. "This should be interesting." Her wearing of the anti-magic deflectors precluded the use of her defensive artifacts, but she had them on in case she needed to ditch the deflector. "I've never liked these things. I prefer to go on offense with my own shit."

"I know how you feel." James ran his fingers over his own deflector. He'd never before used one in his entire career, always trusting in his amulet, but this was one time he couldn't be sure Whispy would offer enough protection. It wasn't a matter of armor or hardening his skin, but his mind and soul.

The deflector wouldn't interfere with Whispy, given that he wasn't a magic artifact, but it felt strange.

"This Lassom fucker is going down," James growled. He tromped toward the reception area where dozens of men and women held guns and waited, their eyes glassy. "Not a big surprise, but he saw us coming," he shouted. "Let me get their attention, and then you all follow up when I make a few opportunities."

"Ready up!" Maria shouted.

The bounty hunters disengaged the safeties on their stun rifles. Several glanced down at the sonic grenades clipped to their tactical vests.

Hiding behind people makes you a pussy, Lassom. You made a big mistake by coming to Los Angeles.

James marched toward the front door with a deep scowl on his face. None of the people inside fired at him. He stopped before opening the door and stared at a man in a Vegas Raiders t-Shirt standing right behind one of the windows forming the outer walls of the office. The mind-controlled Raiders fan held a shotgun.

Given their faces, everyone inside was a victim of Lyle Lassom.

Yes, you can *use force to solve every problem. You just have to know where to apply it.*

"Let's do this shit," James shouted. He charged toward the window, screaming a war cry at the top of his lungs.

None of the people inside moved or reacted until James crashed through the window. Shattered glass shot everywhere and the people inside opened fire, the simultaneous volley deafening. A swarm of bullets pelted him, stinging and bouncing to the ground, where they formed a pile around him.

Near maximum adaptation previously achieved against attack type, Whispy reported, his excitement waning.

James tossed four sonic grenades in rapid succession.

People groaned and collapsed following the characteristic whine. It didn't matter if they were mind-controlled, their bodies still functioned normally.

The bounty hunter grabbed the shotgun from the Raiders fan and rushed over to the other windows. He swung it like a club, smashing the window before rushing to the next to do the same. Soon, glass coated the ground, and the Brownstone Army had a clear line of fire for the stun rifles. As useful as the weapons were, the energy would dissipate when striking glass.

Additional glassy-eyed people with guns ran down the hallway to open fire on James.

The bounty hunters rushed forward, opening fire, a near-blue wall of energy surging on either side of James and downing the other men and women in the lobby. The mind-controlled security turned toward Brownstone's people, but it was too late; person after person fell. It took less than a minute to stun every single person in the lobby, as well as the arriving reinforcements.

The Brownstone Army rushed inside, and half kept their weapons at the ready while the other half began securing prisoners. The lobby area was clear of threats.

Adaptation potential minimal, Whispy complained.

Shay hurried over to James. "That's awful that he did that to those innocent people."

"That shit was just to slow people down." James shook his head. "No wizards or witches in that crowd. Nothing magical or Oriceran."

The elevator dinged, and everyone glanced that way. The doors opened to reveal an empty elevator.

"What's that about?" Shay asked.

The elevator doors closed.

James frowned. A few seconds later, two elves winked into existence on the opposite side of the elevator doors. One elf threw a white energy bolt at a nearby bounty hunter without an anti-magic deflector.

Lachlan threw himself in front of the attack, stumbling back, his anti-magic deflector darkening. Several people fired their rifles at the elves. Their shields flashed when each bolt struck, neither fell.

The second elf raised his hands and started chanting. A wave of wind shot through the lobby, knocking several bounty hunters over.

"The fucking deflectors can't do shit about actual forces," Shay muttered. She yanked out two of her gnome-crafted knives. "These should get through normal shields."

James shook his head. "We can't kill them. They might be mind-controlled."

"Can I mention how boring that is? Let me test a theory, then—something Maria mentioned to me once about a takedown when you weren't around." Shay sheathed the knives and threw a sonic grenade. Both elves crumpled to the ground, clutching their ears.

The sustained blasts from dozens of stun rifles finally made it through their shields, and the elves twitched and writhed as the high-powered bolts pelted them. Their eyes rolled up, and they started drooling.

Maria waved from the corner to James. "We've got this under control. You keep going."

James nodded to Shay, and they ran to the stairwell. Taking an elevator in an enemy-controlled building was never smart. He flung open the door, and they bounded up the stairs. The door at the second-floor landing already stood open, which was not a good sign.

A wide hallway was on the other side, but there was no one there. James stepped inside. The path finally turned again, leading to the senior partner's office.

According to what Weber had passed on to Maria, thermal scans indicated that someone was in the office. Everyone agreed that the kind of man who mind-controlled innocent people would pick the most important office in his building. They weren't attacking directly from the opposite side because they couldn't be sure it was in fact Lassom.

"Aircraft carrier," Shay announced.

"Huh?" James looked over her way, ignoring Whispy as the amulet again complained about adaptation potential and primary directives.

"We've never fought anyone on an aircraft carrier. I was just thinking how we've cleared out office buildings, museums, tombs, haunted forests, and all sorts of other places, but never an aircraft carrier." Shay shrugged. "Would be fun."

James grunted. "We're not military. We've got no reason to fight people on aircraft carriers."

Two Kilomeas stepped into the main hallway from the junction and glared at James.

Shay went for her gun, but James threw up his hand.

"Poor mind-controlled bastards," he muttered.

"Nah," one of the Kilomeas replied, "we're mercenaries. We like getting paid, and this Lassom guy is paying a lot."

Shay rolled her eyes. "What about now?"

One of the Kilomeas pulled back his jacket to remove a

huge gun. "You go for your gun, we go for our guns. It's just like in—what do they call it?—the Ancient West."

"The *Old* West," James corrected.

"Whatever. I don't really give a shit, but we could do this a different way." The Kilomea pulled a set of glowing brass knuckles out of his pocket, and the other did the same.

Shay frowned. "What's all this about?"

"If you want to shoot, we can do that, but I want to see the great Brownstone in action," the Kilomea taunted. "They say you can punch a bastard through a door. I feel like I've been wasting these magical knuckledusters on worthless garbage, but maybe you can provide a challenge."

Moderate adaptation potential, Whispy observed.

James stepped forward and cracked his knuckles. "Let me handle these assholes."

Shay sighed. "This is like Grandfather all over again."

"Maybe. But I'm done talking sooner this time." James charged the Kilomea.

The two huge Oricerans waited, smug smirks on their faces. The first Kilomea threw a wide punch. He landed a solid blow, but James' head barely moved. The bounty hunter's shoulder crashed into the Kilomea's chest, and he flew backward and crashed onto the floor with a loud crack.

James wasn't sure if the noise was from the floor or the mercenary.

The bounty hunter blocked the second Kilomea's punch and knocked him out with a solid uppercut that launched the huge Oriceran into the ceiling, where he left a dent before falling to the floor.

Near maximum adaptation previously achieved, Whispy explained.

Magic I've already run into plus just some straight-up punching, huh? Well, it was worth a shot.

The first Kilomea winced and scrambled to his feet. James marched over to him and jumped into the air to slug him hard at face level. The mercenary's head snapped back, and his eyes rolled up in the back of his head before he collapsed unconscious on his back.

James glanced down at his anti-magic deflector. It was slightly cloudy.

Oh, it was canceling their magic, too. Poor stupid assholes. You didn't even have the tiniest chance.

Shay shook her head. "I think Lyle is depending too much on numbers to win. A man doesn't become a general just because you give him an army."

James pointed down the hallway where the senior partner's office waited. "He was hoping to hide. The cops didn't know where he was."

"Good point. How did Tyler know?"

James shrugged and walked over to Shay. "Who the fuck cares? I don't think I want to know how that guy finds out half the shit he does."

Shay snickered. "Let's go finish thi—"

A bronze sword smashed through the wall and Shay rolled to her side, narrowly dodging the blow. Another sword crashed through and struck James.

What the fuck?

CHAPTER TWENTY-FIVE

The blade didn't pierce James' defenses, but it *did* send him crashing hard into the wall across the hallway, leaving a huge crack.

The bounty hunter let out a low growl and looked up.

Two bronze statues resembling ancient Chinese soldiers ripped through the office walls and came into the hallway, their movements jerky and slow.

Shay scrambled backward and dropped her stun rifle on the ground. She pulled out her gun and opened fire, but the bullets did little more than scuff the solid metal.

"Well, shit," she muttered.

A witch held a glowing wand in the office on the other side of the new holes. James recognized her as May Wu. He'd checked into some of the other bounty hunters who'd gone after the Council before him.

James smashed a fist into one of the statues and managed to knock the heavy metal construct to the ground, but it pushed itself up immediately.

The other statue swung its sword at Shay, and she leapt

out of its reach. "How the hell do we win against statues? Melt them?"

"No. We take out their controller." James dropkicked the statue closest to him and sent it sailing into the other. They clanged together and fell to the ground, splintering some of the wood.

Shit, I better be careful. If these things fall through, they might kill someone. Got to figure out the situation first.

James turned back toward May. "You're a merc now too? Last I heard, you were still a bounty hunter."

May looked at James, her eyes glassy. "I must defend him," she replied, her voice a monotone. "Mr. Lassom told me to defend him. He ordered it."

The two statues disentangled from one another and rushed toward James, their heavy footfalls cracking the wood beneath them.

One of the statues swung its sword. James blocked it with his arm, a loud clang echoing down the hallway. The other stabbed at him. He grunted as its powerful blow struck, but the attack left only a tiny cut. A follow-up attack severed the chain holding his anti-magic deflector. It fell to the ground and one of the statues stomped on it, shattering it into dozens of small, sharp pieces.

James roared and grabbed the necks of both statues. He shoved them into the wall. "Stun the witch, Shay. She's under mind control." He struggled to keep the statues in place as they clubbed him with the backs of their swords and landed hard blows with their free hands.

Shay scrambled for her dropped stun rifle, snatched it off the ground, and fired three quick stun bolts at May. The witch crumpled to the rug of the office, her wand rolling out of her hand and a quiet groan escaping her mouth.

The two statues struggled with James for a few more seconds before they froze and fell on their sides.

James pointed at May. "Get her downstairs. I'm gonna go end this shit."

"Be careful." Shay nodded and rushed over to the fallen witch. She draped the woman's arm over her shoulder and carried her toward the elevator.

James took a few deep breaths and headed down the hall to the large office at the end. He didn't run toward the door, but when he arrived, he kicked it off its hinges. It landed on the ground with an echoing *thud*.

Lyle stood in front of the huge desk dominating the room, his hand on his chest. "You know something? Ever since I came to LA, I've been asking myself what would happen if James Brownstone came after me. I worked through all sorts of scenarios in my mind. Kind of worked myself up over it."

"And what did you come up with?" James rumbled.

"That it's stupid to be scared of you when you're as awesome as I am." Lyle smiled. "You're really scary and people shouldn't fuck with you, but you're known for being tough, not for anything else. You can't win against me, so what reason is there to be scared?" He shrugged.

Adaptation potential high, Whispy reported.

James cracked his knuckles. *Imminent ass-kicking potential high.*

He eyed the unassuming man and shook his head. "You're a complete piece of shit, Lassom. Some of the lowlifes I've taken down are saints compared to you."

"No, I'm a god who is still reaching his maximum potential." Lyle licked his lips. "And you're an arrogant idiot, Brownstone. You had one chance at defense, and you aren't wearing it." He pointed at James' chest.

What? Is this about Whispy?

James looked down and grunted. He'd forgotten about the destroyed anti-magic deflector.

"You're going to go downstairs and kill everyone you see," Lyle said cheerfully. "After you finish them off, you'll go outside and kill every cop you see."

The words repeated in James' mind over and over and he turned slowly away from Lyle, his eyes going glassy.

Kill everyone you see. Kill every cop you see.

Kill, kill, kill.

James growled as rage flowed through him. The armor shot from his amulet, covering his body, and a helmet settled over his head. His blade didn't extend, but the claws on both hands did.

Kill, kill, kill. Kill everyone you see. Kill, kill, kill.

"Destroy them all, Brownstone!" Lyle shouted, laughing. "Show them the power of James Brownstone."

James halted. A long, low snarl followed.

Kill, kill, kill.

Initiating thought filter.

The voice telling him to kill faded to a buzz in the background. James turned around, growling.

Lyle blinked. "Wait." He held up a hand, resting his other on his chest. "Stop." His eyes widened. "Oh, I get it. It's like an anti-magic deflector. I just have to get through its limit."

James took a step forward. "Limit?" He flexed his clawed fingers. "I'm pissed now. There's no limit."

"Go kill everyone downstairs," Lyle commanded, his eyes wide. "Hop on one foot. Throw yourself out the window. Go get me some water. Hum the main theme song from *Ancestor's Quest.*"

James took another step forward, still growling.

"Go to Disneyland. Jump in the ocean. Order a quad-quad at In-N-Out." Lyle shook his head. "No way. This isn't fair. I'm a god. This isn't fair."

"Tell that to all the people you fucked over, you sonofabitch." James raked down Lyle's chest, ripping open his shirt and undershirt and leaving deep gouges. The bounty hunter's attack tore the bone charm from the Lassom's bloody chest.

Lyle screamed and fell to his knees, and James kicked him into a nearby wall. The would-be mastermind fell to the ground, the side of his face bloody, but still breathing and alive.

James growled as he looked down at the charm. He brought up his armored foot and stomped on it several times until it was nothing but a pile of jagged pieces.

Some things just didn't need to exist.

James watched as they loaded Lyle into an ambulance. A single officer sat in the back of the vehicle with him. Without his charm, Lyle was nothing but a two-bit hustler, and the grave threat he had presented was gone. The destruction of the charm released the lingering magic and freed all the other victims. The police and bounty hunters could only wonder how many people in the city had been under the influence of Lyle Lassom.

Shay patted James on the shoulder. "A few minor injuries here and there, but I'm pretty sure Lyle's the only one seriously injured. Maybe you should have given him a healing potion. If he dies, you might not get the bounty. It looked like you tore half his chest off."

"I've got plenty of money." James grunted. "If he dies, he dies. I'll make sure everyone gets paid. I should have just wasted that fucker for what he did. I kind of regret not doing it."

"Think about it this way: now he gets to sit in prison and realize how far he's fallen."

James chuckled. "I didn't think of it that way." He looked over as someone walked their way.

May Wu made her way through the crowd toward Shay and James, a pensive look on her face. "I haven't had a chance yet to thank you and apologize."

James shook his head. "It's not your fault. And I was just doing my job."

"I thought because of my statue magic I could take him. I'm...still getting used to working alone, and I've made sloppy mistakes because of it." The young woman's face darkened. "But it's really not Lassom I wanted to thank you for, Brownstone. It's for taking out those Council bastards. I know my family will rest easier because of what you've done."

James nodded slowly. "They killed one of my guys, too."

May sighed and offered him a shallow nod.

Shay watched the two, understanding on her face.

"Why are you working alone?" James asked. "Don't you have a younger sister?"

May shook her head. "She's given up on bounty hunting. She can't get over what happened, but I don't know what to do other than go after bad guys. Just have to get used to doing it by myself. I'm getting there."

"You don't have to do that if you don't want to." James gestured at the crowd of black-suited agents. "I could have come in here and killed hundreds of people, but I was able to save hundreds instead because of my team. We're always looking for new people for that team, and we could use another witch, especially one who is willing to go somewhere besides Vegas."

"I don't know." May sighed and looked down at her hands. "I have to think about it, and after this, I might want to take some time off. Thanks, Brownstone. I'll let you know." She nodded and turned to leave.

Shay smiled. "That was nice, James. I think she needed that."

"Like I said, we could use another witch, and someone who fought the Council will understand how dangerous shit can be." James stared at the windows he'd shattered earlier. "And sometimes it's not about how much force you use, but where you aim it."

CHAPTER TWENTY-SIX

"Yeah," James rumbled into his phone. "I still kind of wish I had killed the fucker. I know he's gonna rot in prison forever, but I'm still annoyed."

Shay looked over from her side of the bed. James had been talking to Lieutenant Weber for the last fifteen minutes, but she couldn't follow the conversation because of her fiancé's general laconic tendencies.

"Thanks for letting me know, Weber." James turned off his phone and tossed it onto his nightstand.

"What did he say?" Shay asked.

"We got Lassom at the right time," James replied. "The fucker was bragging to those Kilomea mercs about a big plan he had to do some major hostage shit and hide through mind-controlled puppets, including a plan at a stadium. The little piece of shit understood he needed to keep people between himself and others, but he still thought he could get away with it."

Shay rolled onto her side to face James. "Subtlety's a

lost art. If I had a power like that, I'd be using it in ways people would never notice."

"Like blowing up a cartel?" James grinned.

"I said a power like *that*. My ass-kicking ability isn't subtle by its nature." Shay furrowed her brow. "You called me away from the bridal show. I have to admit I'm still having trouble thinking up an epic fucking wedding."

"This shit is hard, isn't it?" James chuckled.

"Yeah. I've got all the bridesmaids figured out, at least."

"That reminds me, I've got another wedding request."

Shay laughed. "By the time this shit is done, you will have planned the whole wedding."

"I want Thomas to be the ring dog. I saw that shit on the internet."

Shay stared at him. "Um, that one I'm going to have to think about." She leaned over to kiss him. "It might have been a few crazy weeks, but I feel like everything's starting to finally calm down. No alien stalkers, no government conspiracies, just us doing what we do. I'll be able to settle into the new semester without too much trouble now."

James grunted. "Yeah, just a nice and simple life—with a few three-headed dragons and mind-control bastards thrown in for spice."

Senator Johnston continued typing as someone stepped into his room and closed the door. "Since my assistant didn't call ahead, you don't have an appointment. I'm a very busy man. Go outside and make an appointment."

"*You* called *me*," replied an amused voice.

The senator looked up from his computer screen to find a Light Elf smiling at him. It was the Fixer, Correk.

"I did at that," Senator Johnston replied with a smile. "I apologize for my rudeness. I have a few things to discuss with you. I don't know if you are aware of the current situation with the Nine Systems Alliance?"

Correk folded his hands in front of him. "My understanding is that they now have another permanent representative on Earth. One pretending to be a human, but who at least your government and a few other key governments are aware of and dealing with."

"Exactly." Senator Johnston frowned. "The reason I contacted you was that I wanted to discuss backup plans in regard to the Alliance. The President has given me his full confidence in this matter. Quite frankly, I'm simply providing plausible deniability, but we all have our roles."

Correk moved over to sit in the chair in front of the senator's desk. "Backup plans?"

"Yes. You're the Fixer, and you're supposed to help all magical beings on Earth."

"Why are you bringing it up now?" The elf frowned slightly.

"Because you can't help the magical beings of Earth if the Nine Systems Alliance turns them to dust by nuking our planet." Senator Johnston gave him a tight-lipped smile. "And it just so happens that helping them also helps us non-magicals."

Correk scoffed. "Do you have evidence the Alliance intends to do that?"

"They were prepared to fire a so-called antimatter torpedo at Earth when we met them." The senator shrugged. "We got lucky that we were ready for them last time and the alien involved was reasonable. Next time, maybe they don't care. They're so damned afraid of Brownstone that they might do something stupid."

"And I'm not saying to do this, but you've never maintained even a brief flirtation with handing him over to the Alliance, right?" Correk raised an eyebrow in question.

Senator Johnston shook his head. "To hell with that. He's a loyal American, and on top of it, if they're that afraid of him, it's a good thing. We don't know this Nine Systems Alliance from whatever random Martians might be out there. Even if we assume everything they say about the Vax is true, that doesn't mean they're good people." He leaned back in his chair. "And so what if they get a little spooked about our magic? From what little they've admitted, they don't have any magic on any of the planets in their Alliance. They associate portals with the Vax and consider them to be very dangerous. Maybe they will end up taking offense to something on Earth and come for us. Right now, the fact that we still have Brownstone gives us leverage to get them to back the fuck off."

Correk furrowed his brow. "You're saying that you want to use Brownstone as a weapon against the Alliance? That's a dangerous game you're playing."

The senator scoffed. "I'm saying a man loyal to his country and planet will defend it. I won't mind pointing him at the Alliance if they get too frisky. That's one of the reasons I've helped him." He raised a hand. "Now, don't get me wrong. I genuinely like the man, but liking someone and using them as a tool aren't mutually exclusive. And now that we know about the Alliance and the Vax, let alone some of the other aliens out there, we have to keep asking ourselves what we'll do if they don't come in peace.

"And what have you come up with?"

"I think having strategic-level magical solutions ready would be helpful," Senator Johnston replied.

Correk frowned. "King Oriceran isn't going to support anything that's a violation of the Great Treaty, or, I should point out, violations of agreements between Earth countries and the Oricerans about the same issues. You're worried about the Alliance, but I don't think you realize that if there was another Great War like on Oriceran, it'd be more terrible than you could imagine."

Senator Johnston pointed to a framed "Blue Marble" Earth photo on his wall. "If Earth goes down, all magical beings on Earth go down with it, even if the Oricerans can protect themselves. There are billions of lives on the line."

"You're misunderstanding." Correk waved a hand. "There are political considerations for both planets, so we should focus on solutions that don't violate our political constraints but are still useful as backups to Brownstone."

Senator Johnston nodded. "*Now* we're getting somewhere. What did you have in mind?"

"The beginnings of a plan. There are just a few items that need to be recovered for it. Ms. Carson has already gotten us some, so maybe she and Brownstone can help with the others." Correk cleared his throat. "Along with a few people affiliated with your CIA."

Senator Johnston folded his hands in front of him. "Tell me more."

THANK YOU for not only reading this story but these *Author Notes* **as well.**

(I think I've been good with always opening with "thank you." If not, I need to edit the other *Author Notes*!)

RANDOM (*sometimes***) THOUGHTS?**

So, my Oriceran Partner in Crime (OPC) Martha Carr has been nudging (read, *harassing*) me about doing a set of stories AFTER Brownstone 18 comes to an end that I'm just not feeling. Once I started the comment above, I realized WAIT A TIC - I CAN'T REVEAL THAT YET!

DAMN!

Ok, two more books and then all will be revealed that (I think) we need to reveal about this side of the Brownstone Family.

If you haven't picked up Alison's tales, you might want to do that. She is NOT (and yet is) a chip off the old blocks of her adopted parents.

Alison has more patience and provides a few more

opportunities for people than James would. However, there *is* a limit to Alison's patience.

It's a family trait.

AROUND THE WORLD IN 80 DAYS

One of the interesting (at least to me) aspects of my life is the ability to work from anywhere and at any time. In the future, I hope to re-read my own *Author Notes* and remember my life as a diary entry.

The Antlers Hotel, Colorado Springs USA - Superstars Writing Conference (Kevin J. Anderson)

I'm in my hotel room, working at the table in the "living" room of the two room suite. My wife and I pretty much need this type of separation for multiple reasons that I won't get in to.

However, it helps keep our marriage happy. I'm a morning person, she is not.

Enough said.

The view out our window is magnificent. Mountains all around and it snowed on our way across a street to get to a restaurant. The swirling snow as it danced down the street in snake-like coils was very interesting. The wind-chill factor cold of about five degrees was NOT an acceptable return on investment.

OK, I will admit it - I am a real wuss when it gets cold. I find it fascinating and delightful—and I find the cold that comes with it a show-stopper at times. I apparently want the beauty without the pain that goes with it. Perhaps I want the cabin-in-the-woods experience without the shivering and the shakes.

Is that too much to ask?

(Personal note: The Antlers Hotel has AMAZING heaters. While the decor is decidedly 1980s rustic and I have NO idea how the heating works, I can tell you that I feel very comfortable admitting their heater can make it like the Sahara in my room.

In the middle of a snowstorm.

And I was raised in Houston, Tx.)

FAN PRICING

$0.99 Saturdays (new LMBPN stuff) and $0.99 Wednesday (both LMBPN books and friends of LMBPN books.) Get great stuff from us and others at tantalizing prices.

Go ahead. I bet you can't read just one.

Sign up here: http://lmbpn.com/email/.

HOW TO MARKET FOR BOOKS YOU LOVE

Review them so others have your thoughts, and tell friends and the dogs of your enemies (because who wants to talk to enemies?)… *Enough said ;-)*

Ad Aeternitatem,

Michael Anderle

OTHER SERIES IN THE ORICERAN
UNIVERSE:

Other series in the Oriceran Universe:
THE DANIEL CODEX SERIES
I FEAR NO EVIL
THE UNBELIEVABLE MR. BROWNSTONE
SCHOOL OF NECESSARY MAGIC
THE LEIRA CHRONICLES
REWRITING JUSTICE
THE KACY CHRONICLES
MIDWEST MAGIC CHRONICLES
SOUL STONE MAGE
THE FAIRHAVEN CHRONICLES

OTHER BOOKS BY JUDITH BERENS

www.ingramcontent.com/pod-product-compliance
Lightning Source LLC
Chambersburg PA
CBHW050231110726
47898CB00007B/2100